THE RANDY

This edition published 2020
By Living Book Press
Copyright © Dorothy Lucy Sanders Literary Estate (1948)

First published in 1948 by The Australasian Publishing Co. Pty Ltd.

The publisher would like to give a huge 'Thank You' to the author's family for their assistance in making this book available once more.

ISBN: 978-1-925729-92-4 (paperback)
         978-1-925729-93-1 (ebook)

A catalogue record for this book is available from the National Library of Australia

THE RANDY

The Story of a Mystery Ship

BY

DOROTHY LUCIE SANDERS

CONTENTS

A portion of The Randy has already appeared in The Bulletin as a short story under the title of Jeem.

CHAPTER ONE

THE UNKNOWN BAY

JEEM was dead and nothing that the Police Commissioner and my father could say about it could alter that fact. I saw him dead. His sallow face was an unearthly green-grey; his sodden clothes were bunched up round him and his wet hair lay black and draggled over his brow. I saw him lying like that on the rocks up at the bay, and so did Joe and Sven and Ilka though they denied it... denied they even knew me... I pleaded with Joe, the tears in my eyes. I couldn't believe that he would pretend that he didn't know me. It was cruel beyond belief. As I looked up into his kindly, puzzled face in the Commissioner's office I just couldn't bring myself to believe that Joe was doing this. That Joe, who'd spent endless days swimming and fishing and even shooting a little up at the bay, should be looking at me with that strange stare and denying that he'd ever been to the bay... that there'd ever been a ship called the Randy.

...And Joe's commanding officer, speaking in that slow American drawl, testifying that Joe had never been absent from duty; that during the time I said the sailors had been up at the bay they had, in fact, been at sea.

I couldn't understand it, not any of it. I still can't... But perhaps if I go over it all again, start at the beginning and put every detail down, I may remember something, some little thing, that will help me find the answer...

The story of the mystery ship Randy and of my long quest for her, which finally took me all over the seven seas, began on the shores of the west coast of Australia three or four years ago.

Here there are thousands of miles of sealine edged with flat grey country. It is as lonely as the forgotten places... the places of the earth where prehistoric men may have lived but where only a few have cared to make their dwelling since the beginning of modern times; a dry deserted country with no deep watercourses and few creeks, and those mostly salty or brackish. The sea, that lies green and blue along its shoreline, looks calm and gentle enough but it has moods that, though rare, can be devastating. Along the coast, from Rottnest Island in the south to the far north, you will hear stories of ships wrecked upon the reefs, of crews that disappeared and left no traces of their going.

And yet this seacoast is the home of all my dreams. Here the blueness of heaven is only excelled by the blueness of sea. Near the southern extremities of this coast the white man first settled. Then in the far, blue north he found the greatest treasure of the sea... pearls. And in the exploitation of that treasure came the brown and yellow men so that now the pearling ports have some, if not all, of the glamour of the exotic east.

At least that is how I thought of things when first I came across the Randy.

Four years ago Blackman's Bay was still the limits of seaside settlement in the southern province of the State. When my father built a cottage there he said the beaches were the finest in the world and that some day soon the world would discover them. Penn's Jetty, Benson Beach, North Beach and most northerly of all the settled beaches in this province... Blackman's Bay. Here were wide stretches of fine yellow sand, protected from the rough surge of the Indian Ocean by the straggling reefs that are a fisherman's paradise.

I was only fifteen the day I set out for a long walk along the water's edge. My father and mother had taken us out to the cottage for the summer months and it was a day upon which I felt I could not endure the company of any member of my family. I had been quarrelling with my parents. That is... as much as a fifteen year old *can* quarrel with his parents. They said they were tired of my day-dreaming, of my pre-occupation with the sea and of my absorption with books. I had not tried to make them understand how I felt about the great sweep of the sea and the strange glittering beaches that I peopled with creatures of my own imagination. I left them to their own occupations and sought the loneliness of the sunlit sands. Here I could imagine bygone kingdoms, perhaps of aboriginals, or even of sea kings and mermaids who knew and loved these long shores with their piles of jumbled rock and their distant white horses. Here I could dream of the ghosts of the Dutch brigands from the shipwrecked "Batavia," and wonder if, after all these three hundred years, they did not still keep a secret tryst with the sea and reefs that had spelled their doom.

I had walked for a long time and gone much further north than I'd been before. Then I came to the bay.

It was a little inward curve of sand between two rocky promontories with tall, thick bush coming right to the edge of the beach.

Out to sea the reef curved in, too, so that the bay was as calm as a land-locked lake.

The water was a mysterious translucent green and

as I waded through it and swam in it, my eyes were fascinated by the beauties of the sandy bottom, the secret fastnesses of miniature merman kingdoms. I resolved then that I would come secretly to the bay every day… only in future I would bring something to eat and some fresh water in a bottle.

On the third day Jeem came to my bay.

I had had my swim and was lying half dozing in the sun when I heard a whistle. I looked up, and there about thirty yards away was Jeem, standing just outside the belt of trees and idly throwing pieces of cuttle shell at the water's edge. He was about fourteen or fifteen and even at that distance, I could see his olive skin and realize that his eyes were dark, perhaps black.

"Hallo there," I called, pulling myself up to a sitting position. Jeem walked over to me and I could see at once that I was going to like him enormously and not mind his being on my beach a bit. Sure enough he had black eyes, glowing like coals in a thin, sallow face. His hair was a bit too long, and looked as if he'd been cutting it himself. I remembered afterwards that he was pretty shabby altogether. His trousers were too long—down to his knees in fact—and his shirt was a faded blue dungaree with more than one tear in evidence. But these things didn't seem to matter beside his fine and friendly face. It was the finest face I'd ever seen on a boy, strong and clean, and I knew at once that he was rare enough not to think a fellow's fancies about the beach peculiar.

"Where'd you come from?" he asked.

"Back there." I nodded my head in the direction of Blackman's Bay. "D'ye mind my being here?" I asked, and I remembered that afterwards I thought that was a funny question for me to ask. But, somehow, I suddenly felt that this was his beach after all, and that he had lived there a long time.

"No," he said, squatting down in the sand beside me. "It's lonely here sometimes." He spoke with a queer accent. It sounded to me as if it might be Dutch. Not that I'd ever known anyone from Holland, but for some strange reason I associated it with Jeem. That is, until I looked at his feet. The structure of his face and body was fine and narrow, but his feet didn't fit in. They were broad and flat, and the texture of the skin was dark beyond sunburning. They were the kind of feet we used to call blackfella's feet at school, and I immediately thought that Jeem might have aboriginal blood in him. I didn't mind that. I liked it. That's what made him different: made him look and sound as if he belonged here, where white men seldom came.

"Where do you live?" I asked.

"In there," he said, looking in the direction of the bush.

"Are your people there?" I asked him. "Have you got a holiday cottage? What do you do for water?"

"Oh, there's water if you know where to look for it," he said. He looked at me with his dark, friendly eyes. "My family have been using a little stream there for over a hundred years."

"A hundred years!" I said incredulously. "Nobody lives for a hundred years."

"Silly ass," he said without anger. "My father's father, in his time. That's what I mean." He paused a moment. "They're all gone now. I'm the last of them."

"Do you mean you live alone?" I asked, with mixed envy and disbelief.

"Well, for the time being, anyway," he said a little sadly. "When the folks down there..." and he nodded his head to the south, "find out, they'll come hunting for me and that'll be the end of all my peace and happiness."

"But what do you live on?" I asked excitedly.

"Live on! Good heavens, there's fish, and kangaroo and I've got a yam patch back there. Why we've never lived on anything else for a hundred years." This sounded a bit tall to me, but it also sounded happy and exciting and I decided not to ask any more questions just yet.

"Do you want to go fishing on the reef?" Jeem asked. (That was the way he pronounced his name and I liked it.)

"Do I what!" I said. "Just lead the way."

And Jeem did. First of all he showed me a miniature cave in the northerly end of the rock spit where he had fishing tackle hidden. There were some lines made of twine and some unbelievably ancient hooks. "Picked up by my father long ago," said Jeem. But more interesting than these, were some spears with stone heads which Jeem said his father had made and which were his sole weapon before he found the fishing lines. Then we began to follow the direction of the rock promontory out to sea, stepping high in the shallow water and sometimes leaping from rock to rock. It must have taken us nearly half an hour to work our way out to the reef by that path of shallow waters and jutting rocks, but at last we were seated high on the weed strewn jags of the reef.

"We've two hours before the tide comes in," said Jeem. "The water doesn't cover the reef entirely, but we'd have to swim home."

"Have you ever had to do it?" I asked him.

"Lots of times," he said. "Could you?"

"I'd give it a good fling," I said with conviction. And as I can swim pretty well, I don't think I was boasting. Then we settled down to the business of fishing. We were pretty lucky, and I suppose that made us feel more friendly still towards each other. Perhaps that is why Jeem told me his secret...

"Nobody knows where we get our water from," he said mysteriously. "Many people have come here hunting for our water hole, but no one has ever found it," and he led me a little way along the reef to where a particularly large cluster of rocks rose up out of the water in circular fashion. In the centre of the pool formed by the rocks, the water was fresh.

"An underground spring," Jeem said. "And it comes out here." I could hardly believe my eyes, but the water was pure and fresh, as I can show anyone to this day.

"Do you always have to come out to the reef for your water?" I asked.

"No," said Jeem. "My grandfather discovered this water first, and took a direct line with that crop of rocks you can see over there," and he pointed to the southern promontory. "Just where those rocks meet the sea is another spring," he said. "You have to put your cup into the sea to catch the fresh water. That's why no one else has ever found it."

Too soon the daytime fled by, and I had to think about going home. Jeem showed me many more strange and exciting things about the reef, and afterwards, when we'd waded back and had another swim, he fetched me water from the stream that came out just below the beach level.

I was late home that day, but I never said a word about the bay or Jeem. That was all part of my own private world; I thought and dreamed about it by night, and each day I set out for the bay and a day of glorious sunlit pleasure.

"Where'd you go all day?" Mother asked. "It isn't natural for a boy to go off by himself all the time."

"I'm not by myself," I replied at length. "There's another boy I go swimming with up at the beach."

"What's that?" said Dad. "Someone camping on the beach? There aren't any cottages from here on."

"That's what everyone thinks," I replied. "This chap lives up there. He's never lived anywhere else in his life."

"There isn't any water up there," said Dad in a contrary tone.

"Yes, there is," I said.

"There's a water hole the half-blooded tribe used to use," said Mother, for once on my side. "They say that no one has ever found it."

"That's only legend," said my father. "You know what fishermen's tales are."

I nursed my secret knowledge of Jeem's springs and let my family put what construction they liked on my mysterious companion, so long as they didn't stop my going to the bay. And though they often talked of stopping me, they never did.

About ten days after Jeem and I first met, we were lying sunbaking in the dunes, when three American sailors turned the corner of the southern promontory and sauntered along the bay.

"Cripes," said Jeem. "What's these?"

"Americans," I said. "Haven't you seen Americans before?"

I watched them through half-closed sleepy eyes as they came towards us. I wondered what had brought American sailors so far north. Then as they came closer, I suddenly realised that I'd seen these three sailors before. One day my brother and I had gone down to Benson Beach for a surfing carnival, and there were a lot of Americans about. These three men had been sitting together a little apart from the crowd and after a while we struck up a conversation with them. I remembered the one called Joe particularly, because he seemed to be the leader of the three. He had a face so full of life, with dancing, blue eyes that seemed to snap with laughter, and when he smiled, you saw a perfect set of white teeth. Joe was not quite as tall as the other two... Sven and Ilka, they were called, and I think they must have been of Nordic extraction. They were big and fair with light blue eyes, and though they, too, were full of laughter, they hadn't got Joe's charm or Joe's knack of spinning yarns that were thrilling and realistic. We asked them what boat they came from, and Joe told us that they were submarine men, but that they really belonged to the Randy. The Randy acted as a supply ship to the submarine, and it was of the Randy that Joe always spoke. They laughed a lot when they told us about her... it was almost as if the boat was a live thing to them, and as if so much that they had had to do with her had been gay and adventurous and lively. We wanted to know everything about her and Joe said... "Say, don't you kids know there's a war on?" I remember telling him that as we were only kids, we could hardly be spies and I couldn't see what harm it would be to tell us a bit about her.

Well, that started them off. The Randy was not only a supply ship but a pirate, they told us. Her job was "pirating" for Japanese and German supply ships in the Indian Ocean and they told us some of the jobs she had done, some of the fierce encounters they'd had. I know my hair was fairly standing on end some of the time. And Sven and Ilka laughed at everything Joe said. Their teeth flashed and they threw sand balls at one another to punctuate their delight in the exploits of their ship. I could have listened to Joe all night.

And now here were the same three sailors miles from Benson Beach, walking up the sandy stretch of our bay.

"Joe!" I cried excitedly as I jumped up and ran down to meet them.

"Why, if it isn't Ginge himself," said Joe. Everyone called me that because of my red hair, but I didn't mind it coming from Joe. "And what are you doing here, and who's your buddy this time?" went on Joe.

I told him quickly about Jeem, and the bay and then in turn I asked him the question that was uppermost in my mind.

"What are you doing here?" I said.

The three sailors exchanged glances and then as of one accord threw themselves down on the sand.

"We might as well tell the kid," said Joe to the others. "He's O.K."

Sven and Ilka both said "Okay," and then Joe told me that they were A.W.O.L. They'd got mixed up with some New Zealanders down at the port, and had missed their sub, and the Randy.

"Now," said Joe. "If we'd reported to the U.S. Navy as we are supposed to do, we'd have been put in barracks till the Randy and her pal came to port again, and then once aboard we'd be up for as much time as if we'd been loose all the while. So we might as well be free and make a good time of it. Do you see?"

Somehow I was a bit shocked that they were A.W.O.L., and my face must have showed it, for Joe suddenly reached forward and cuffed my head in a friendly way.

"Aw, it's okay, kid," he said. "Every sailor misses a boat sometime or other in his career. Could I help it if a Kiwi clouted me unconscious and Sven and Ilka stayed around to help me? Anyhow, if we did report to headquarters, we could be shipped away in any old tramp. You wouldn't have us miss the Randy, would you?"

That seemed reasonable to me, and put things right, and once again Joe leaped back to his own special place in my estimation.

"Tell me and Jeem some more about the Randy," I cried eagerly.

"Okay, okay. But what about something to eat? We are fair famished."

Jeem and I looked at one another in dismay. There was nothing in the tucker bag.

"I'll tell you what," said Jeem. "I'll go out to the

reef and spear some fish and maybe bring in a cray or two. You get that old kerosene tin full of fresh water and start a fire going."

I was all for making the fire the way Jeem had shown me with a twirling fire-stick but the Americans got in first by producing a box of matches.

"Slow," Joe drawled, looking at my fire-stick. "Very slow. I believe in the modern way of fire making." And in a few seconds he had a good blaze under the tin.

It didn't seem long (though Joe said it was a heck of a time), before Jeem was back, and half a dozen crays were turning pink in the tin, and some big sea mullet were smouldering in the ashes. The sailors had a quick swim in the sea while the fish were cooking, and after we had all eaten our fill, we lay chatting and half dozing in the sand while the afternoon wore on.

It was decided that Joe and Sven and Ilka should camp in the bush for the time being, and for an hour we had a fine time building them a bush humpy in Australian style. Jeem didn't offer to take them home, so no one suggested it, but they couldn't have been better off anyway. They seemed snug and set for the night when I left for my long trek home, but I promised to be back long before midday, loaded, I hoped, with some of my mother's stores secretly removed from the kitchen.

That was the first of many wonderful days. We swam and fished and even tried a little futile shooting with a revolver that Ilka carried, but we didn't hit anything. In fact, Ilka had better luck with the knife which he could use as effectively as Jeem could use the stone headed spears. Sven, too, could whittle any shape out of a bit of cuttle shell or a small piece of wood. But of the three, Joe was the best. Not that Sven and Ilka weren't wonderful comrades. They were, but to my mind they were not to be compared with Joe.

And the yarns Joe could tell!

When we grew tired of fishing or swimming, we would lie in the sand, and he would tell us about the Randy. She had tramped the northwest seas, he said, for many years before the war, and then she was called into service. I lay many an hour and listened to him enraptured, and only when the sun sank level with the ocean and everything—heaven and earth—was blood red with the rays of the setting sun, would I sadly drag myself away from them and dawdle the long way home.

After a while my father and mother began to worry, and wanted me to stay at home.

"There's something wrong with the boy," they'd say.

"A boy shouldn't go off on his own like that; he's getting thin; his eyes are strained; he looks wretched."

Talk, talk, talk! I'd never been happier in my life, though I suppose I was a bit thinner because of the long walk every day to the bay. Nothing they could say would make me stay at home. The Randy had captured my imagination, and Jeem and I were blood brothers. Everything one of us seemed to do or say, the other approved of; while the Americans told us of a life at sea in one of the most daring of all sea-going ships, and of the hectic life ashore in foreign ports, where the fame of the Randy had always spread before her.

The Randy! What magic that name was in my ears! I had never been to sea, never seen a ship at close quarters. But from our summer holiday cottage I had watched many a vessel coming and going through the Roads. Many and many a day, and often in the evening, I had sat upon the sands gazing across the Indian Ocean, dreaming of ships and of a life at sea. It irritated my father almost beyond endurance for he declared that my longings were only those of all boys of my age, and that he would never allow me to be a sailor.

Joe drew us so perfect a picture of the Randy, that I felt that I would know her at once if ever I saw her. Before these holidays I had longed in a nebulous kind of way for a life at sea, but now knew that I would never be happy until I boarded the Randy. My day dreams all turned upon that point. I thought continuously of how I would search for, and one day find, her.

That is why, on the last day of our holidays, as I set off up the beach I knew, when I saw a ship coming over the horizon and turning into the Roads, that it was the Randy. Joe had said that she would be in any day now, and that then their troubles "would really begin."

But it was something more than premonition and the fact that she was expected soon, that made me recognise her. As she came inshore I could see that her lines were unusual, and that there was a gallant swift look about her that I'd never seen before in any of the vessels passing along the Roads.

No, it was the Randy, and my heart was filled with a mixed feeling of pride and excitement, and a kind of sadness. The Randy had come to port. Tomorrow we were shifting back to our town house, and there would be only Jeem alone on the bay.

I was suddenly appalled by the thought. If the end of the holidays was a tragedy for me, what would it be for Jeem? He would be absolutely alone on the beach. No American sailors, no Randy, no me. Suddenly the bay lost all its lustre. I saw it empty and forlorn, with Jeem standing alone on its wet sands.

I looked out to sea, and there now seemed something

purposeful and forbidding about the Randy. She was coming to port, and with her the submarine to take Joe and Sven and Ilka away forever.

I rounded the southern promontory and, for a moment, I thought the bay was empty. Then in the distance, I saw the sailors wading on to the shore by the northern rock path from the reefs; they were carrying something between them. Where was Jeem? I started to run across the sands, and as I drew nearer, I could see quite distinctly that it was a body they were carrying. It must be Jeem! It couldn't be anyone else! I saw them stagger over the last few rocks and deposit their burden carefully on a flat rock. Joe bent over it for a minute. He straightened up just as I approached.

"Look out, here's the kid," said Sven. Joe turned quickly.

"Take it easy, kid," he said. "Take it easy."

I pushed him aside, and stared down at Jeem. I had never seen anyone dead, but I knew at once that Jeem was dead. It was the unearthly greyness. Suddenly, the back of my head felt as if it would burst apart. I know I clasped it in a kind of physical and mental torment. Words wouldn't come. I could only stare at Joe.

"Take it easy, take it easy," he kept saying, and I felt his strong hand on my arm. There was nothing for me to do but stand and stare at his kind, brown face. There were tumult and horror in my mind, and a kind of frenzy. Even when I looked away from Joe to the sea, I could see Jeem's grey face and the black, draggled hair. It was horrible.

"It was out at the reef," Joe was saying. "We never saw it. Just heard him give a cry, and he went over backwards. We never moved... thought he would come up and shake the hair and water out of his eyes... you know the way he used to... but he didn't come up. Sven realised first and he shot in after him. He had to dive twice before he got him... there's a hole as big as your fist in the side of his head... he didn't drown... he hit a rock..."

I pushed past Joe. I had to see Jeem again... He lay in a strange dumped way, with his clothes all wet and bunched up. And under the left side of his head a pool of blood and water was widening... I turned away and ran across the sand to the edge of the bush. I threw myself on the ground, and sobbed as if my heart and head would burst.

I don't know how long I was there, but in the end, I fell into a kind of doze, a half sleep that robbed me of my senses, yet did not shut out the whirling world.

It was fairly midday by the position of the sun

when the three sailors came and sat down beside me. My face burned, and my head was beginning to ache.

"How are you feeling?" Joe asked.

"He's been lying too long in the sun," said Sven.

I felt the touch of Joe's strong hand on my arm, and responded to the brusque kindness of his voice.

"Take it easy, son." I sat up and, drawing my knees under my chin, I rested my aching head on them.

"We buried him where he'd like to be," said Joe. "We gave him a seaman's funeral. We've buried him at sea."

I lifted up my head and stared at him.

"You can't do that," I said. My voice was cracked and quavery in my ears. "The police! Someone will have to know he's dead. He might have people somewhere. The police will have to know." I suddenly felt frightened and alone, and desperately sick in the pit of my stomach. Joe and Sven and Ilka looked at me, and then at one another. Sven and Ilka nodded to Joe, and he began to talk again in that slow soft drawl, a note of patience and persuasiveness in his voice.

"Listen, kid. Jeem never had any people. He lived here alone, and has lived here alone for years. We found his humpy one day ages ago..." and they exchanged looks again. "We knew then that Jeem was on his own. You'd be right about the police, kid, if this was any ordinary case. But it's not, and we want you to see it our way, Jeem was killed by an accident, but it's going to be hard to prove it... with the Randy gone to sea..." He stopped and looked out to the west where the Randy was now far down towards the port.

"There she is now," he said with a strange warm note of pride in his voice. We all stared at her as she rode, lovely and impatient, at anchor. Waiting, one supposed, for a pilot boat to take her into port.

"You see, kid," Joe went on. "We've got to get away tonight. We don't want to lose our sub, again... she'll be coming up there behind the Randy. It isn't as if it would do any good... as if it would bring Jeem back."

It was all as clear as daylight to me. Joe and the boys had to go now if they were to rejoin their own ship. If they told the police there'd be delays... things they called post mortems... inquests... there'd be nothing but trouble for Joe and Sven and Ilka and none of it would bring Jeem back.

No... no... no. Jeem had had an honourable funeral. A seaman's funeral, and there he should rest in peace.

After a long while, the sailors told me they had removed their camp shelter and were ready to push on.

"Come on, kid," they said. "Let's get going." In silence we passed round the rocky pile to the south of the bay, and not one of us looked back, though for one mad moment, I thought if I did, I would see Jeem standing there, alone, throwing lumps of cuttle shell into the sea.

I don't know how I got home, or just when or where I said goodbye to the boys. All I can remember, is my splitting headache, and a feeling of stumbling against the sun and the glassy stare of the sea. Somehow or other, I got back, and I can remember my mother saying...

"Goodness, what's brought you home before sundown?" And then she started up, and I guess I must have looked pretty bad. "What's the matter, boy?" she asked sharply.

"My head," I mumbled, and somehow pushed my way to the back verandah room. Blindly I felt for the bed and, crawling on it, put my splitting, burning head on the pillow.

I don't know how many days I was unconscious, but it was long enough to have muttered all about the bay... of Jeem... and of the three American sailors.

Then began a hard time for me. People came to ask me questions. I had been too ill for my family to move back to our town house as they had planned, and now it was not an unusual sight to see a car with a Perth number parked outside our house, while someone was inside, either questioning me, or in the dining room in consultation with Dad.

The doctor was the keenest of all with his questions. He wanted to know the colour of Jeem's eyes, his height, how his face looked when he was dead. Time and again he came back to the colour of his eyes. He would pop the question in suddenly while saying something else. It was no good. I couldn't hold out against them all, and I had no idea how much I had told them when I was unconscious. The doctor was hard at it one day, when I suddenly gave in and burst into tears like a girl, and then I told him the whole story. He listened without once interrupting, but never taking his eyes from my face, and never losing that slightly disbelieving air that I found difficult to bear. From time to time he would rest his hand on my wrist and I knew he was taking my pulse. When I had finished, he walked to the window and stood silently staring out for a minute or two. At last he turned around.

"Boy," he said. "I want you to forget this whole holiday. Forget the bay; forget you've ever been ill. Now, how are you going to do it?"

I stared at him blankly.

"I'll tell you what," he said, coming over to the bed

and sitting on the end of it. "You like the sea, don't you? How would you like to go to sea?"

"Go to sea?" I cried. "Why, that's all I've ever wanted to do. But Dad'll never hear of it. He grows angry every time it's mentioned. 'Every silly fool of a boy wants to go to sea.' That's what he says."

"Well," said the doctor. "I'll see if I can influence him... and I think I can. But only on one condition, mind you. You forget about the bay. Start thinking about going to sea."

And with that he left me, but I didn't even let myself hope that he'd be able to influence my father. They'd *never* let me go to sea.

The rumour got around the little seaside town as to why I'd been ill, and one day, I saw the local constable talking to my father on the side verandah. I was lying on the lounge below the drawing room window, and I could hear what was said. I was frightened, and I listened desperately to catch all I could.

"But we found his camps..." I heard the policeman say. Then later: "We found where someone had been spearing and cooking fish."

"Oh, quite likely," I heard my father reply a little testily. "He's quite capable of doing all those things."

Shortly after that the constable went away, but the

next day a detective came out from town. This time, I had to come into the dining room and tell him the whole story from beginning to end. He was like the doctor in that he repeated some questions over and over again. "Where were the patches on Jeem's shirt? What was the colour of Joe's eyes? Did he wear boots or shoes?" When I had finished, he looked up at my father and said...

"I'm not doubting that you and the doctor are right, but it's remarkable. He never falters or makes an error on a detail."

All the while my father had said nothing, and for the first time I realised that no member of my family had asked me any questions for a long time, and that none of them had mentioned the constable's visit the previous day. Perhaps the doctor had cautioned them to help me to forget the whole business. Thinking of it was bad for me, I know, because after both the visits, I was sick, and had throbbing headaches.

Several days later, my father and I, with the doctor, had to go into the city to see the Police Commissioner. When we got there, we waited for a few minutes in a waiting room, and then a policeman opened an inside door and invited us to come in. The doctor and my father went in first and I followed, very frightened and feeling sick in my head. Once inside, I didn't feel so bad. The Commissioner's room was big and airy, and he was a tall, kind looking man, rather like the doctor, only not so stout. He and my father and the doctor were shaking hands, and that little conventional act quietened my palpitating heart more than anything else.

"We're not really doubting your diagnosis, doctor," the Commissioner was saying. "But in this job... especially when there are rumours at large... we have to check every detail."

With that he turned and looked at me, and asked me, not unkindly, if I would like to sit down. I was glad to do so as my head had begun to ache again, and I was afraid I might get dizzy.

"Well, boy," he said. "We don't want to worry you with the whole story again. We've got it here in every detail." He pointed to a file on his desk, and then turned to the doctor.

"You will agree there are some extraordinary coincidences in the details of the story," he said. "Particulars about the three Americans and the waterhole, for instance."

"Quite, quite," said the doctor. "I'm just as anxious as you to have my diagnosis verified."

"Well," said the Commissioner, "a submarine is just

in port with some interesting people aboard. Three men who we know were on Benson Beach at the surfing carnival. I want to see if this boy knows them."

He rang a bell on his desk, and immediately a door opened and a policeman appeared. "Ask the Americans to come in, will you, constable?" he said.

A second or two later, Joe and Sven and Ilka came into the room with a fourth man who was an officer.

I stared at them unbelievingly. It was Joe, and yet... and yet... there was something different. I thought I knew every line of his face, and yet to-day, there was an indefinable difference. And Sven! And Ilka! I stared at them, and suddenly I felt my eyes mist over as if there were tears in them. I could hardly see my three friends for the blur before my eyes. And I knew why. Joe and Sven and Ilka were staring at me vacantly, as if they had never seen me before.

Then I realised that every eye in that room was on me, and no one had spoken since the men came into the room. They were waiting for me to say something. I felt lost and hostile. I felt high up on a mountain peak alone in a terribly misty world, miles from any-where, anyone.

"Joe," I began. But nothing more would come.

"That's me, kid," said Joe. "What's up, buddy?"

"Joe, don't you KNOW me?"

"Well, buddy... I'd like to know you, but I don't really..."

Joe not know me! It couldn't be. I turned to Sven... the same puzzled look. Ilka? Not one of them! Not one of them KNEW me. It couldn't be true! The top of my head began to hammer, and all their faces blurred together. Suddenly, it seemed, my mountain peak became higher and more remote, and mists rose about me.

"Lieutenant Macon informs me that these men have been at sea in their submarine for the last six weeks." The Commissioner's voice seemed to come from a great distance. "As far as any known authority is aware there is no such ship as the Randy, except in a yarn one of these men told two kids on the beach at Benson some time ago."

"Quite." I heard the doctor's voice, but the rest of his words were lost to me for, suddenly, the mists closed over me...

Slowly the room began to take form around me again. Only it wasn't the Commissioner's room. I was lying on the floor of the anteroom, and a policewoman was kneeling beside me, dabbing my forehead with something cold.

"How's that?" she said. "Feeling better? You fainted,

you know." I saw the door open and the Americans come out and, crossing past me, file through the opposite door. Joe looked back for a minute, and there was a flicker in his eyes, as though, somehow, he was sorry. Did he recognise me after all? What was the meaning of that look?

The door of the Commissioner's room was ajar, and I could hear the doctor's voice.

"A very unusual case," he was saying. "I suspected what the trouble was immediately the father told me he was given to day-dreaming and wandering about the beach alone. It is the case of a lonely boy romancing and becoming so engrossed in his imaginings that his fantasies become his real life. Split personality, we call it. Forced back into everyday life by the approaching conclusion of his holiday, his mind feels it cannot bear to take farewell of the dream playmate. So he imagines a death. Thus, in his mind, he rationalises the parting. Of course, he crowns it all by getting a very serious touch of sunstroke."

The three men were coming through the door, and the policewoman helped me to my feet. My father came forward and took me by the arm, and for the first time as I looked into his face, I saw a great kindness there, and I was sorry for the trouble in it.

"And your solution, doctor?" the Commissioner asked.

"A life of action," said the doctor with emphasis.

"The lad's going to sea," my father said. He looked down at me and pressed my arm. "As soon as he's fit."

I looked at him, and the words choked in my throat. I was grateful to him. But I knew I had not dreamed it all as they said, though I knew I would have to let it rest at that for the time being. The doctor's diagnosis had brought about my father's change of heart, and for that I was thankful. But I knew, too, that I would have to find the Randy myself, if I was ever to know why Joe had pretended not to know me, and why at the last moment he had relented by just that tiny flicker in his eyes as he went out the door.

CHAPTER II

CASTAWAY

WHEN my father put me to sea, my family thought that that would be the end of my daydreaming. A life of action... that's what they said would cure me. But they were wrong. I never could give up the idea that somewhere in the world there was a ship called the Randy. The love I had for that ship persisted through all my waking moments, and I never saw a tell-tale wisp of smoke on the horizon without thinking:

"Maybe that's the Randy."

But, of course, it never was. I knew that I would recognise her if ever I saw her again, even though my father and the doctor said the only time I ever had seen her was in my imagination. But they were wrong, and one day I was to prove it.

Well, going to sea wasn't much fun at first, though I certainly had plenty of action... mostly in the kitchen carrying slops for the cooks. That's the way they'd said it would be, so I couldn't complain. They'd only say they'd warned me.

But I never wanted to give it up, even when the

weather was most foul, and the cook in his worst mood; even though I had no one to talk to, and every seaman thought the only way to teach a boy the ways of the sea was by pushing him around. Somehow sailors are different when they're at sea.

But there was always the ocean. Always the creak and groan of the ship as she rolled; always the smell of paint and tar; always the distant rim of the horizon, somewhere beyond which were the big cities of the world, and the smoke and smell and racket of harbours in distant lands.

It was on our second run in the Timor Sea that we were chased by the Japanese. We were caught one late afternoon in a sudden mist, and when it cleared, we found that we had them on our starboard. There was nothing to do but run for it, and hope that night would fall fast enough to cover us. We were out of luck, because a half an hour later, a small Japanese gunboat appeared on our port side. She was faster than we were, but already the sky was darkening, and as night falls in a few minutes in these latitudes, we were saved. Fortune was both with and against us. The next day we ran into another armed Japanese ship, but she wasn't fast enough to catch us... just fast enough to hang around. It almost looked as if we were ringed by the enemy.

Whichever way we went, we struck the Japanese, but never once did they force us within range of their guns. Our real danger lay in the fact that we were running out of fuel. Things had been so bad in the north, that we had had to drop some of our reserves of fuel at a port where the need for it was desperate.

At this juncture, fortune gave a hand on our side. An American submarine came to our assistance, and gave us directions to one of the island bases, where there was a supply of emergency fuel.

The next day we sighted the island in mid-afternoon. We came close in along what looked like a deserted shore. The Japanese never bivouacs on the sea shore. He always puts a barrier of jungle between himself and any enemy who might come up out of the sea. This gives him the advantage of keeping his presence a secret, but it gives a small allied ship the advantage of being able to come in close under the jungle topped shore, where the Japanese can't see him or find him with their guns.

We had no reason to believe that any Japanese had located the island, but we had to take the usual precautions. The skipper knew the layout of the little cove, where the stores were guarded by a tiny garrison. The idea was to bring the ship in about two miles further up the coast, then lower a small boat which would take a minimum landing party ashore. The party would then make its way along the beach and get a spy's view of the cove. If all were well, it would signal the ship. If not...

The landing party consisted of the mate, a deck hand called Jim Browning, and myself. We came into the shore without any trouble, and after beaching the boat in a manner which made it safe and partly concealed—as well as easy to launch again—we made off up the shore under the mangroves. The place was as silent and deserted as the grave. Not a leaf stirred or a twig snapped as we ploughed our way through the damp sand to the ridge of the sand-dunes which should over-look the garrison, and which should, by rights, be patrolled by a sentry.

As we neared the summit of the hill, we crept in more under the mangroves.

"No guard seems to have spotted us," said the mate. "So let's hope the Japs haven't either."

After a minute he spoke again.

"Too quiet," he said. "I don't like it."

We crawled on our bellies the last few yards, and lay looking over the sand down onto the shattered store houses below. "Cripes," said Joe Browning. "They've been here."

I felt the skin on the back of my neck crawling.

"You get back to the beach," said the mate to Jim. "Signal the ship. Use your handkerchiefs. Don't shout. Keep under the trees and get the boat eased into the water. Ginge, you stay here and pass any signal you get from me on to Jim. I'm going down to have a look at what happened to the garrison."

It seemed only a matter of seconds before the mate had gone one way and Jim the other, and I was left alone, half buried in the sand on the top of the hill. I felt pretty sick. When I looked at the ship lying so near, hugging the shore under the jungle cover, I wanted to run for it, but, of course, I didn't. Instead I watched the mate, and wondered how men came to be so brave. It didn't seem anything to him to go down there where every tree, every mound of rock, might hide a waiting Japanese. I began to feel in the eerie silence that they were all around me. I felt so that I couldn't look at the ship any more for fear that I would up and run for it. Instead I kept my eyes on the furtive figure of the mate, as he made his way in a zigzag path down the beach towards the wrecked huts that I could see quite clearly. Soon I lost sight of him altogether, though I had already had a signal from Jim to tell the mate to make for the ship at once. We had precious cargo aboard, and the skipper wasn't taking any chances.

I suppose it was half an hour before he came up again. He came out of the mangroves just to the north of me, so I had no time to send the signal to him. He reached me first.

"They must have had a fight for it," he said. "There's no sign of anything alive. The stores have been taken. And men have been killed there. I could see where they'd been buried. Japs did the burying," he went on, grimly. Then he looked at me rather closely. "How you taking it, kid. Still game?"

"I'm game," I said, but I guess I looked pretty sick on it. The mate was a decent sort of chap, though. He pretended not to notice.

We got down to the shore, and Jim had the boat in the water, and without wasting a word or a minute, we jumped in, and the mate and Jim began to pull away to the ship which had already hoisted anchor.

We were already about half way to the ship when a Japanese reconnaissance plane flew right over our heads. At the same moment two torn and tattered figures appeared on the beach. They waved and cried to us with a kind of desperation, that fairly turned my heart. The mate shipped in his oars and looked at them. Two frantic figures of white men calling to us for assistance! At the same time the plane circled low again, and began machine-gunning the ship. From the Captain's bridge came the single message. "Hurry!" We knew what that meant: the ship had to be moving to escape serious drilling. If we didn't hurry, she couldn't wait for us.

The mate was barely silent a minute.

"This little boat carries emergency stores. It means life to those two chaps."

I looked at him wonderingly.

"Aren't you going back for them?" I asked. I felt suddenly sick in the pit of my stomach.

"The skipper won't wait for us. He can't."

"The whole ship's at stake," put in Jim, "The bombers will be over any minute now."

"So it looks as if we'll have to leave those two chaps if we want to save our own skins, eh?" asked the mate.

"Whatever you say, sir," said Jim.

"What about you, Ginge?"

"What you say, sir," I said, and then blurted out. "But for Heaven's sake, don't leave them behind!"

As we put about, I heard the skipper hallooing through his megaphoned hands, and the mate answering. I could see the ship clearly, and in a minute, I knew she was moving out to sea.

We pulled in towards the shore rapidly, and before we even looked up and took stock of the two men running towards us, we set to work to beach the boat and cover it well from observation. Before we had finished, the men were upon us, and giving us a hand to remove the stores. They were Americans, survivors of the garrison, and had been hiding in the swamps and foothills for close on ten days. Both were thin from days of starvation and from fever. It is certain that, if we had not come to their rescue when we did, they would not have survived much longer.

Four of them had escaped to the hills, they told us, but two had already died from fever. They were the last left to tell the terrible tale. Most of the Japanese had gone, they said, but there was still a small party on the north side operating a radio-transmitting station. The Americans had had neither the strength nor the ammunition to do anything about the station, but they had managed to maintain a fairly consistent observation of its activities as well as try to keep a lookout for an Allied ship that might either be in danger, or be able to take them off.

We followed their advice and moved higher up the hills to camp. The fumes off the swamps, quite apart from the mosquitoes and insects, made living on the lower level absolutely impossible. Higher up the air was good enough, though the mosquitoes were still bad.

The mate rationed out some quinine all round, and we went to work on some tinned meat. The Americans told us their story and it wasn't good hearing. Both men were sick, and their nerves were torn to shreds. Fever leaves a man's nerves in a bad way.

The next day the mate put Jim to watch the Japanese at the station, and I kept a lookout to the south, while he tried to fix up the Americans so as to let them relax a bit. But it seemed as if they couldn't rest. They walked about with quick, nervous movements, and talked incessantly.

The only disadvantage of the camp up in the hills, was the length of time it took to get to the shore. It was because of this delay that the two refugees had so nearly missed us.

After a day or two, when they were rested and better for the quinine and food we had given them, we started on a new plan of campaign. Two of us were to put in the day at the lower level of the beach so as to be nearer contact when a rescue ship arrived—as none of us doubted it would.

I liked my days on the shore. I liked my surreptitious swim under the lee of some rocks; and I liked lying in the sand looking out to sea. I liked to dream that when a ship came to rescue us, it would be the Randy.

One day I was taking my turn with one of the Americans, and I began to tell him about the Randy. I was lying with my eyes half-closed, looking between the palms at the flat blue sea with its long rollers curving into shore.

"Gee!" I said. "If only the Randy would come swinging round that headland."

"The Randy?" he asked. "Never heard of her."

"No," I said. "But you will."

And that's how it began.

I told him about the Randy just as if I had known her all along, and somehow I think he liked listening. It was very dull lying there on the beach, not daring to run openly into the surf or to sprint across the sands, except under cover of the mangroves. And the insects were a constant irritation. I found it easy to talk as I watched the blue sparkle of the little waves way out from the shore, and the foam of the white horses as they came rolling up the beach.

I told all of Joe's stories, and then I began to tell some of my own. I'm afraid I invested the Randy with an even greater power and glory than Joe had done.

And the American picked his teeth with a twig and listened.

When we climbed up to the camp that night, I heard

the men talking to the mate.

"Thought you said it was the boy's first ship at sea."

"Well, so it is."

"There's not much he doesn't know. And what about this Randy he's so full of? That's a ship he knows from stem to stern."

"Hey, Ginge," called the mate. "What's this about the Randy?"

So I began to tell him, and soon they were all listening. The next day I had to stay at camp with Jim and the other American, and they got me telling them about the Randy, too. Soon it became almost our complete pastime.

One night we were sprawled on our bush beds, and one of the Americans laughed.

"Say," he said. "I never knew any ship could get into so much trouble and always get out of it with so much credit. Some ship!"

I fell suddenly silent, and nothing they could say would make me go on. The next day I had to take watch on the beach with the mate, and after we'd had our quick swim in the surf, he asked me how I had first come to know about the Randy.

For a few minutes I felt I couldn't say anything, for I had been feeling terribly miserable ever since the

American made the crack at me the night before.

Then I looked up and saw that the mate was watching me, and that his eyes were filled with kindly understanding.

"Most of the stories I have made up," I confessed sadly, then I looked up and said almost fiercely. "But there *is* such a ship, and it was Joe first told me about her. And once I saw her coming into Fremantle."

The mate looked out to sea, and then I saw him beginning to draw little figures in the sand.

"Who said there wasn't any such ship?" he asked.

After a little while I began to tell him about the bay. When I saw that he not only believed me, but that he knew how I felt about it, I went on and told him the whole story. I told him about Jeem and about the day we had gone to the Commissioner's office. For quite a long time he was silent, and then he sat up and hunching his knees up under his chin, he wrapped his arms about them and looked at me closely.

"Ginge," he said. "It doesn't all add up. Either you *did* imagine it all, or there's something more behind it that neither you nor I can see at the moment." He was silent for some time, and I said nothing; only watched him while he half closed his eyes as if in deep thought.

"You've certainly got an imagination," he went on, "but I don't think you are as cock-eyed as all that. You say that as Joe went out the door he did give you one flickering look of recognition? Well, that's the clue. Boy, I believe you stumbled onto something with those Americans, and they had to shut you up."

"But what?" I cried in mounting excitement.

"I don't know, and neither do you," said the mate. "We'll have to wait until we find the Randy... or maybe Joe... to know the answer to that one. Your father fell an easy victim to that psychology talk. He'd already got a fixed idea about your day-dreaming... and the doctor probably had a bit of a leaning towards that modern stuff, too. It all fitted in nicely for anyone who wanted to shut you up."

I began to pour the sand into little cupped mounds around me.

"If only I could find the Randy," I said.

"You will," said the mate. "And if ever I get there first, I'll be asking a few questions myself. For the time being, you'll have to be patient. I know that those things that Joe told you about her were real, and so are some of the stories you've told us." He turned his head and looked at me again. "You see, Ginge, you've made her exist in our minds. You've created a special kind of Randy for us all. I've got a perfect picture of her in my mind. She's a beautiful ship. Something I'll always think of as what a ship should be like."

I looked at him. Was he making fun of me? But his eyes were very serious, and I knew he understood how a chap who hankers after something feels.

"Gee," I said. "She's a wonderful ship. Lovely as a dream."

Then I caught his eye, and we both laughed.

"You know, Ginge," he said. "It's the best thing that ever happened to us to have a story teller in our midst. It's passed the time. And that's not the first time that's happened in history. You go right on telling us tales about the Randy. Only remember when you've finished... it is only a story. Don't go to bed really believing yourself. That's what makes a fellow miserable."

After that I told my stories far into the night, but the mate always ended things by saying...

"Someday you must write them all down, Ginge."

We were a full month on that island before we were taken off by a Catalina.

One early morning we were making our way down the hillside, when we saw her flying in from the south. She'd come in low from the sea and the mate said at once that she'd been sent especially for us.

"The old tub must have got through after all," he said. "See how she knows not to show herself high up above the island. She's come in from the south at low level—and what'll you bet she lands right alongside the beach where we landed?"

And so she did.

We were near enough to the camp to hear the shouts of the others and know that they had spotted her too. All we had to do now was to cover the distance in as short a time as possible.

It seemed only minutes before we were on the beach. Then before we could get the boat afloat, the others had joined us, and a moment later we were rowing full strength for the aircraft.

"Nice not to have to do any packing," said Jim Browning, and those were the only words spoken as we pulled for our lives.

What a moment that was when we skidded through the sea and suddenly felt the pull as the Catalina left the water, and we were airborne!

The Americans told the skipper about the Japanese transmitting station, and he assured us that that would be taken care of.

"You chaps relax and forget there's a war on," he said. "We'll settle those chaps. Have some coffee?"

Everything that followed after our rescue seemed like a dream to me.

To begin with, we were landed at a big American base.

What a strange miracle was that! Here was a place that a few months before had been an uninhabited strip of jungle. Now it was a mechanised city complete with electricity, drainage, roads and a teeming male population. There must have been thousands and thousands of men passing through that "city" each day and week. But I never saw any women, and on the map there wasn't even the mark of a jungle village.

The mate and I went to hospital with the two Americans. We had some injections, and started right in on a diet of atebrin. After a day or two, the Americans who were being treated as nerve cases, were sent to another base. We weren't in hospital long, and, once outside, we found that everyone took great interest in us.

People came from all over the place to see us, especially a couple of war correspondents, who were looking for a story. In a few days, we saw half a dozen more of these chaps, and they told us they were writing the story of how we went back to the island so as not to leave the castaways. They made a lot more of it than we thought it was worth, and they took a number of photographs which they intended to send to their papers in America. There was nothing that they didn't want to know about the island but, truth to tell, there was very little we could say. It was just an island like all the others around. We couldn't tell them anything of the heroic stand the garrison had made or of the terrible time the survivors had had before we arrived. That was their story... and we left it to them.

One thing did seem to come out of this publicity: the fact that the Americans had been much nearer nervous collapse than I had dreamed, and the Randy stories had really served a good purpose in helping pass the time.

"You see, Ginge," said the mate. "That's what I really meant when I said the Randy's deeds exist now. It was the Randy that helped to keep those men sane."

When we were fit again, the mate and Jim and I were at a loose end, and the C.O. sent for us.

"We can't get you away to Australia for goodness knows how long," he said. "But we want crew for a boat going into the Pacific right now. If you take it, you'll have to sign on for the trip, but you must choose for yourselves. How about it?"

Well, I knew what I wanted to do, but I could see it depended on what job they could offer the mate. He wouldn't go on the deck. But it seemed they wanted a second mate, and it was a ship of twice the tonnage of our old boat, and the mate was pleased. Better still, I was to be his offsider. No more cook's galley for me. Jim Browning elected to wait for a boat to Australia.

Well, she was a dirty ship, like a lot of others in those days that were doing too much work in too little time. But she was fast, and her crew were competent seamen.

We didn't sight land till we came into San Francisco. We had come straight across the Pacific, and the trip had been good and uneventful. There might have been no war for all the trouble we met on those tranquil seas, but we found plenty to bother us when we reached port.

We had no sooner heaved to and got the hatches up, than the boat was besieged by reporters. The mate and I were heroes all right, and our coming had been foreshadowed by those very papers whose correspondents we had met at the base. I couldn't get the drift of things at first. There were people thronging round, cameras snapping and lights flashing. But over and over again came the question. "Where did you get those yarns about the Randy?" or "Where's the Randy now?" "What's the latest about the Randy?"

What did they want with the Randy, I asked myself. I was suddenly overcome with the foolishness of all those stories and I went away and leaned over the ship's side and stared at the oily water lapping against the unpainted sides. The mate did the talking. I felt miserable and unhappy again.

When the tumult and the shouting had died down, we were left alone to get on with our work. The crew were looking at us out of speculating eyes, and we felt pretty foolish. We were the only Britishers aboard that ship, and we weren't sure how the others would like all the publicity.

By nightfall, the papers were out with the story, and the mate brought a huge bundle of them up to where I was standing, watching the shadows lengthen across the reflection of the great bridge in the water.

"Here, look at yourself!" he grunted, as he threw them down at my feet, and then, taking the top paper off the pile, he squatted down on the deck beside me. A little sheepishly, I took another paper, and there was my face staring out at me! I suppose it's natural for a fellow who's never had his photo printed before—let alone published as large as life in the middle of the front page—to feel a bit excited about it. At all events, I started to read as quickly as I could, even though I wouldn't have liked anyone but the mate to have seen me doing it.

It was the third paper that knocked all the fun out of it. I don't know to this day who the chap was who wrote the account in it—although I tried hard enough to find out afterwards—but there must have been something vicious in him. He'd taken the story and made it seem as if I'd told it all just to show what a good fellow I was. He'd put in things I'd never said, and hinted at things I'd never thought, and, by and large, he'd made the Randy and me sound very cheap indeed.

I felt so sick I couldn't speak, but the mate sensed something and came and looked over my shoulder. Before he'd finished reading, I'd made my mind up and stood up abruptly.

"Where are you off to?" the mate asked, standing up too.

"To find that reporter and choke his lies down his throat," I growled, but the mate swung me back by the shoulder.

"You can't do it, Ginge!" he said. "Don't you see? There'd be a brawl and they'd write that up too, and you'd look even cheaper. No, let it die. You'll do the Randy no good by that sort of thing!"

Well, that stopped me. What he said was true, of course, but I still would have liked to get hold of that reporter. For days afterwards, I felt ill when I thought of him and of what Joe would say if he ever saw that paper.

But the people made me feel better. They came

aboard and pressed all manner of invitations on us, and as soon as one lot would move on, another would appear. We were heroes all right, and it looked as if there was nothing we could do about it.

"Come on," said the mate. "Let's have some of the fun. They want to give us a good time. Well, let them!"

You've got to give it to the Americans. When they open their doors they open them wide. It was as if they gave us the whole of San Francisco. We ate and drank and drove in motors. We met people and made speeches and listened to speeches. We went to shows and to the races. We bowled out into the country in fleets of cars, and we slept in the home of a millionaire. It was all like a mad dream. It raced past at such a pace that I was afraid to rub my eyes for fear it would all vanish.

And though we almost drowned ourselves in the goodwill and hospitality, every time the mate and I saw our pictures in the papers, we would squirm. Our own faces looked sadly and accusingly back at us.

"There's lots more heroic deeds in this war that'll go unheard of and unsung," said the mate.

"What's made them take this one up so keenly?" I asked.

"I think it's the Randy," said the mate slowly. "She's taken their imagination too." He paused a moment while I looked at him wonderingly.

"She's a wonderful little ship," he added thoughtfully. Then he looked at me. "You know, Ginge, with all this publicity, you'd think she'd hit the headlines somewhere. Somewhere there must be somebody knows where the Randy's plying."

"No. There's a war on, isn't there?" I asked.

"Yes," said the mate musingly. "But you'd think someone would come to light with something more about her than you've said. After all, there are American boys sailing her. You'd think some proud mother would up and say her boy was on the Randy."

There was a silence between us for a little while.

"Maybe you've come to think there isn't any real Randy after all," I said.

"No," said the mate still thoughtfully. "But there's something doesn't add up. I'd just like this Randy to turn up, for once."

I turned on my heel and went away. Was the mate, too, beginning to believe that I had made up everything about the Randy?

The thought only added to my longing to find my mystery ship. Perhaps I had made her greater, smarter, braver than even Joe had done, but I could not forget that morning I had seen her come over the horizon and ride gently but purposefully down the Roads to Fremantle. I had wanted the Randy for her own sake. Now I wanted her because I had to prove to the mate that she really existed. I was even beginning to doubt myself. Maybe I wanted her badly because my own faith in myself was slipping. They say that if you say a thing often enough you come to believe it yourself. Maybe I was getting that way with the Randy.

A day or two later, when the sensation had begun to abate somewhat, we found we had a little more time to ourselves, and the mate suggested to me that we get someone to take us over the big shipyards that were turning out new ships at the rate of about one a week. We'd heard about them and we both thought we would like to see one of their vessels.

It was no trouble getting someone to take us over. We were still sufficiently in the news for our wishes to be commands.

Well, I don't suppose I'll ever again see anything like those shipyards. They made one great city of themselves. Steel and iron works, carpentry shops, workshops of every kind. Noise, blast and heat with men bending over machines and others hurrying here and there. And beyond all, the yards where the vessels under construction were literally growing before one's eyes, like Jack's beanstalk. It was almost unbelievable!

Towards the end of our tour our guides told us that they had been asked to take us to the owner's office, and we suddenly found ourselves confronted with the prospect of meeting D. W. Burnett, one of the biggest ship-building men in the world, and a millionaire to boot.

I don't know how the mate felt about it all, but I know that I was nervous. I need not have been. He was a small dapper man, very human, with wise eyes and a face full of kindness.

He told us a lot about the new ships he was building, and showed us plans and prints. He wasn't playing down to us, because the mate knew ships, and could talk as well as anyone on that subject. I didn't have their technical knowledge, but I knew that this was a heaven-sent opportunity to learn about the things that interested me more than anything else in the world. Something in me felt happy and satisfied when I saw some of his illustrations of ships he had built, and was going to build. Soon I had forgotten the greatness of the man with whom I was talking. As he turned the pages, his eyes seemed to light when mine did, and standing there, poring over ships new and old, I knew that he and I, the great and the little, both knew what was lovely about a ship. And it wasn't always the way she was built... I don't know what it was... Partly her build, I suppose, but partly too, the spirit that was in her.

We turned the pages slowly. And then, suddenly, it was there! Without announcement, without even premonition of what the folded pages held. It was a picture of the Randy!

I stood a moment with my eyes nearly leaping from my head. A great lump of triumph rose in my throat. There she was, silhouetted against the white of the paper... the ship I had seen the day that Jeem died. The ship Joe had told me of! I put my hand upon the page for fear it would be turned and looked up at the mate. He must have known what I had discovered, for he bent his head in sudden and renewed interest, and then I realised that Mr. Burnett was watching me closely, with almost a look of triumph in his face.

"Yes, there she is," he said.

"The Randy," I said.

"I built her," he said.

"They said there never was such a ship," I almost panted.

He laughed.

"Well, she doesn't bear that name... that's why."

"What is her name?" asked the mate.

The shipbuilder shrugged his shoulders.

"I don't know," he said. "It's a long story. Come with me, and while I take you a little journey to show you something, I will tell you about that ship the lad has claimed. She's just XN217 in the records."

He took his hat from the coat-stand, and went to the door.

"Come along."

We went outside, and entered his car, which he drove himself. None of us spoke for a little while, for we all felt that we were going to see something out of the ordinary. Then we turned along the water front, and as we went, he talked to us of the Randy.

"I built her twelve years ago," he said. "When I'd finished her, I knew she had something different, something a bit special about her. She was rakish, in a way. As though she were destined for adventure. I had a friend... a very close friend... an Australian." He stopped for a few minutes. "You can see now why I was interested in you two chaps. Why I asked for you to come to my office. Because of my Australian friend, all Australians are welcome to me... but when I read those stories Ginge here had been telling about the Randy... I recognised the ship, too."

"Well, you know," said the mate tentatively, and with an apologetic look towards me. "I'm afraid Ginge has a pretty good imagination. Most of those stories he cooked up..."

"I know," interrupted Burnett. "It wasn't the stories of the exploits that made me so sure it was my ship. There were very apt descriptions of her, and there was more than that to it. Those stories were about a ship that had been in the trade in the northwest of Australia before the Americans took her over. Well, that's where XN217 went. That's where my Australian friend, Captain Fitzgerald, took her. You see there were too many coincidences."

"I see," said the mate. "And can we know how you came to let her go with this Captain Fitzgerald?"

"Just that, being friends, we had many ideas in common. When Fitz saw the ship, nothing would stop him, but he must have her. He was the head of a fairly substantial pearling firm, and they bought her from me. She sailed out of here with his name... Fitzgerald... but, as that was not afterwards listed in Lloyds Register, he must have changed it. But I could never find a name for her myself, so she just stayed 217."

"And what happened to Captain Fitzgerald?"

"I don't know," replied Burnett. "But if you ever come across the Randy, you might try looking on the bridge."

"But isn't she U.S. Navy now?" we both exclaimed in one breath.

"So I understand," said Burnett. "But there are occasions when even Navies cut through red tape, you know. We probably took over the Randy on loan at first, because things were desperate in the north of Australia, and the British and U.S. Navies had to make many quick adjustments. I think that the Randy went over to work with our submarines, captain and all. But maybe you can tell me more about that than I already know."

I shook my head.

"Well, never mind," he said. "I'm going to show you something now that'll make you understand why your ship remained just 217 to me."

We had turned the car away from the water front, and followed a little limestone road which cut off a headland, and which led to a tiny cove.

We got out of the car. The wind was blowing off the sea and had the tang of salt in it. I felt it curl through my hair like cool fingers. We walked a little to the headland and looked down to the cove below us.

"There she is," said D. W. Burnett.

It was the Randy's small sister! I stared with unbelieving eyes. A little yacht, shining new in the sun, rode gently at anchor. She was lovely as a dream.

We stood and looked, but none of us spoke. It seemed to me as if my heart had quivered. Was there ever a ship as lovely as this? Her bow came up out of the water like a swan. Her long lines were low and sweeping and though she was swift and keen, she was a gentle peaceful ship, too. The water sparkled and shone around her, but I couldn't find words to say what I thought.

After a while the mate spoke.

"I've only seen the like of her once before."

We both looked up at him sharply.

"Ay," said the mate. "It was in my mind's eye. Now I know there *is* a Randy."

I knew that the mate, too, had found a dream-ship, and if the great Burnett had once lost his to his Australian friend, he was now showing to two more Australians the ship that the other had inspired. And though she was a little thing, not meant for the tramping northwest trade, she had class and beauty.

Looking at her, I knew that I would not cease my hunt for the parent ship. I guessed it would not be here in America that I would find her. It would be somewhere in the blue north of Australia.

CHAPTER III

CAPTAIN FITZGERALD

WE left San Francisco in a Liberty ship bound for Sydney and home. At least, as Sydney is in Australia, it was in a sense home. But I dreamed of a destination beyond Sydney... it was the distant West coast where the breakers rolled long and white on a quiet shore. There, somewhere in those waters, I would solve the mystery of the Randy. It was there I would discover what was the secret of the bay, and what had really befallen upon that day when Jeem had died and I had been taken ill with sunstroke. When I dreamed about these things, I was not merely indulging in wishful thinking. I was sure that if Captain Fitzgerald was still at the helm of the Randy, it would be for the very good reason that he knew the seas north-west of Australia like the palm of his hand. What more likely than to find the ship and the skipper who had learned every harbour and every hidden atoll in the days of peace, now seeking and destroying the enemy in the places they knew so well.

We had a cargo of aeroplane parts, and knew that

one sight of us by the Japanese and up we'd go. But none of us worried. It's funny how reconciled to danger one gets. When the winds roar up out of the south, there is enough in the plunging of the ship and the creak of the plates and the bitter cold to keep one's mind on those things and nothing else. Lifeboat drill seems fantastic; just an example of the skipper's wish to make life difficult.

And life was difficult on that voyage. At least, it was for a boy with red hair, for those Americans never left the subject of my hair alone. But I had to stick it, and stick it I did, though often times I was longing to be away from that ship, and aboard that other, where I knew there would be so much adventure that there wouldn't be time to worry about the colour of one's hair.

We drove well down into the South Pacific, and one day, were hove-to off a small island, which I guessed was in the New Hebrides. We were taking cases aboard from lighters, but there didn't seem very much to take and it was likely that we'd be away before morning. One of the Americans leaning over the rail whistled, and then turned to us.

"Say, you boys thought we were going to Sydney, didn't you?" he asked. "Where do you think we're taking those packing cases? Dampier!"

"Dampier!" I cried in excitement. "Are you sure? How do you know? "

"I just heard a remark or two from those fellows on the launch," he said. "And I put two and two together. But what are you looking so pleased about? Dampier's a dump."

"A dump?" I almost shouted at him. "What do you know about Dampier? Have you ever been on the north-west coast?"

He spat eloquently into the water.

"I'll say," he said. "I was there when they bombed her. Not a gun in the town, and seventeen flying boats sitting targets in the bay. Women and kids screaming in the water. Dampier... I'll never forget it."

I wrinkled up my eyes against the sun. I tried to see in my mind those flying boats lying there in the bay, and the Japanese bombers coming in low, and the townsfolk standing there helpless along the shore. Dampier, the little pearling port, had never known that it would one day be a key refuelling place for planes escaping from the Netherlands East Indies. It had never thought to line the marshy edges of its bay with guns, or to hide amongst the sandhills those weapons for defence so necessary to save the live cargoes fleeing from the invasion in the north.

Yes, Dampier—stinking, little north-west pearling port though it was—had had its hour.

And now Dampier was our destination!

If there had never been a ship called the Randy, if there had never been a day upon which Jeem died, nor three American sailors who told tales to two boys on a lonely sea shore, I would still have thrilled at the prospect of going to Dampier. And thus it was that I stood on the deck waiting impatiently for the incoming tide and the day when finally we did come into that bay in the remote north west of Australia. I stared with burning interest towards the mangrove swamps and the sandhills where, they said, lay buried those whose bodies had been taken from the water after that fateful day when all the aircraft had fallen easy victim to the Japanese.

Yes, it was a little town, and perhaps some of its glamour was gone from it because there were no pearling luggers lying along the shore. But there was something vivid about it still. And the brown faces and the gay tropical colours gave it a distinctiveness, that was not to be found anywhere else in Australia.

The homes of the white bosses stood forlorn and empty, for most of the white population had been sent south. The club and the hotel were officers' quarters now, and the little port had a military air.

Except for the brown faces. They were here as in all the sea cities of the east—brown and yellow, inscrutable, patient. The place was the meeting point of many races: here in Dampier there were to be found more coloured people than there had ever been white. Here they lived against a background of incredibly blue skies and the deep secretive blue of the sea.

When I went ashore, I was strangely exhilarated. I gazed curiously at the skeletons of wrecked luggers and the salt encrusted litter of the pearlers that lined the edge of the bay. I gazed out over the clear, turquoise water and wondered what were the secrets of the deep that those skeleton luggers had known. What of the sharks, the giant rays, the octopus? What of the strange beauty of the ocean bed where men had crawled leaden footed in their search for pearls?

And the thrill of the Randy grew greater in my heart because I was here, where she must have been, and I was looking into the glorious depths of the waters where she must have sailed.

For there was something more than the lure of Dampier drawing me on. I was looking for news of the Randy.

I wandered through the dusty white street of the native quarter, and I stopped to see some Malay women making their nets. I pointed up towards the hill where the prim and elegant latticed bungalows of the white men stood silent and empty.

"Where are they?" I asked. "Have all the white men gone?"

"Not all," said one of them, looking up at me. "And some not come back any more." She pointed to one or two houses and gave the white owners' names. "Gone to the war and killed," she said. Her companion spoke to her in her light lilting tongue, and they laughed together, and looked up at me knowingly, each showing the tip of a very pink tongue.

"Captain Fitzgerald!" the first woman said. "He live in that big one. He will come back one day. Chinaman up there keep the house plenty clean case he come anytime."

"Captain Fitzgerald!" I cried. "So this is his port." Within myself I was crying. "I knew it! I knew it!"

The women laughed and giggled together again.

"Captain Fitzgerald a very bad man," the women said again, and they went into paroxysms of laughter. They would tell me no more about him, but laughed uproariously at my anxious questions. They rolled their knowing brown eyes, and wiped their pink tongues over their bottom lips. I knew by the quick way they looked at me and at one another and giggled that they did not really mean "a bad man." And yet, even if they had meant it, I doubt if I could have brought myself to believe it.

I turned up the road that led to the hill, leaving the bay behind me and the smell of refuse and littered crab shell that dominated the centre of the town. I passed one or two of the wooden bungalows with their wide latticed verandahs, and their empty, lost look, and I came to the one that the coloured women had pointed out to me.

It was a larger house than the others. When I mounted the steep path and stood on the steps, I saw that it overlooked all the bay and the town. I felt that the house shared something of Captain Fitzgerald's personality. It had an air of superiority and command. I felt a strange delight as I sensed this, and I knew that I approved of it. "This is just the place for the man who bought the Randy" I thought.

The house was shut up. If Captain Fitzgerald had a Chinese servant waiting for his return, he was not in. The silence about the house was proof enough that there was no one there. I sat on the step with that silence behind me, and it was for all the world as if the house itself knew I was there, and was glad of it.

"What is it about me that the house knows?" I wondered, and then, half-smiling, knew the answer. "It is my love for the Randy. The house and I know that somewhere in the world there is the Randy and that with her is Captain Fitzgerald."

I jumped up with a start, for I realized that I did not really know if Captain Fitzgerald was with the Randy at all. She was U.S. Navy now... more than likely there would be an American skipper. I turned and looked at the house again, and it had a bland superior look. It almost told me that I need not worry... that all was well with the Randy... and Captain Fitzgerald.

Excited by a new sense of delight in Dampier, and what I was discovering there, I made my way back to the town. I couldn't tell even the mate that a house had spoken to me. I laughed as I went because I, too, knew it was ridiculous. Nevertheless, I had a feeling that Captain Fitzgerald and the Randy were together and that somewhere here in Dampier, I would hear news of them. I almost turned and waved my hand to the house.

Well, I got my news of the Randy all right. And with it, there came a new figure into my life. I knew that henceforward, the Randy would not be alone in my thoughts. Part and parcel with her went the skipper, Captain Fitz, as everyone in Dampier called him. The fantasy of the one must include the fantasy of the other, for I understood now, as a result of all that I saw and heard in Dampier, that the two were inseparable.

I asked all sorts of people about the Randy.

Yes, they knew her. They would laugh and look knowing when I spoke of her. They knew her by that name in these waters. Someone, I forget whom, did tell me that she had another name, but that no one referred to her by it. It was an elegant, unusual name, he said. He could not remember it. But someone had called her the Randy when she first came into the bay with Captain Fitzgerald.

"She looked like she'd suit the old Cap'n," the man said. "There was never any other ship came into this port looked like her. She had a fine rakish look about her. 'Why, say, have a look at the Randy that Cap'n Fitz has brought himself from America,' they said up at the club. And Randy she's been ever since."

I asked all around the bay after her, and always the dark people and the brown people and the little yellow children would laugh and flash their teeth and say...

"You know Captain Fitz? When he coming back?"

Yes, they all knew the Randy, and they all knew Captain Fitz. I pieced together the picture of them both by talking to all the different types of people I could find. One of the officers, sitting on an old lugger when the tide had gone out, told me the things people had told him after he had come to Dampier. He too, had never seen the Randy or Captain Fitz, but he said you couldn't be in Dampier twenty-four hours without someone telling you something good or bad about Captain Fitzgerald.

I could see that it would be his friends who spoke well of him, and that if he had enemies, it was because of his wealth and the dominant position he held in the town. It would be his enemies who spoke ill of him.

In my mind's eye I could picture the fine big man with the deep, resonant voice that people spoke of. I could imagine him and the Randy slipping out to sea in the pearl grey of a tropical morning, destined for harbours in strange places that no man in Dampier knew.

I asked some half-castes on the beach for news of the ship, and one of them had sailed with the Randy.

"Where did you go?" I asked.

He laughed, and laid his finger along his nose.

"Up in the Banda Sea," he said. "Cap'n Fitz say 'Come on, you fella, I'm sick of this white fella place. You come fishing with me.' 'Boss,' I say. 'You going to take lugger fishing?' 'No fear,' he say. 'Randy sick of this place, too.' So we go alonga Cap'n Fitz up in the islands."

"But what did you do there?" I asked.

They all laughed a great deal. They poked one another, and winked and laid their fingers along their noses.

"Fishing," said the half-caste.

"But fishing for what?" I asked.

"Fish," he said, and they laughed in their strange guileless way, their dark eyes rolling, and their white teeth showing shining and wet in their mouths.

"Up in the Banda Sea" the half-caste had said. What pictures of lovely atolls lying curved about their lagoons that phrase brought to me. And as I dreamed of them lying still in the great tropic seas, I could understand why it was the Americans had asked Captain Fitzgerald to come with them, and keep his command of the Randy. No man knew those archipelagoes, those uncharted passages between coral fringed islands, like Captain Fitzgerald. He knew them like the palm of his hand. Who better than he to take his ship where only he knew she could go?

The tales they told of Captain Fitz and the Randy in Dampier! They thrilled me because at last I knew that my own fantastic dreams had some foundation in reality, and even the tales of Joe did not excel the one that was on the lips of everyone when I asked for news of the Randy. It was the story of the last time she had come to port.

I could see by the way some people spoke of Captain Fitzgerald that it was very easy to believe good or ill of him. The half-caste had said they had gone fishing in the Banda Sea. There were others in the town who told me that no one knew what the Randy did when she went slipping away to the horizon. No one knew what she sought, gliding through still, tropic seas, among little known islands. And there were those who always talked about the archipelagoes in the north in subdued tones. There, they said, is where the Japanese ran their illicit pearl shell trade in the days before the war.

They did not have to tell me—for I guessed the suspicion in everyone's mind—about the "nefarious" doings of the Randy in the northern seas. I could see at once how it was that, with one accord, the townsfolk could believe the worst of Captain Fitz. His personality was too big for them. He was too grand, his gestures too wide, his laugh too hearty... his purse too full.

They told me that, after the Japanese came into the war, Cap'n Fitz gave up the sea for a while in order to control the petrol supplies for the north. Everyone in Dampier knew that the government had arranged with Captain Fitz for the placing of big petrol dumps. No one knew where those dumps were, but everyone knew that Captain Fitz was busy about the business.

The townsfolk of Dampier are full of laughter. They may not have been big enough really to understand a man like Captain Fitz, but they knew how to laugh against themselves. They told me with gusto how the pearling luggers had all disappeared out of the bay one night. At sundown they were there, and in the morning, they had gone out with the tide.

Where had they gone? Even listening to the story, I responded to the fear in that query. The Randy too, had gone. Where had the Randy gone? Not fishing in the Banda Sea surely? And without her skipper, for Captain Fitzgerald was about his petrol business in Dampier.

Sitting there on the sands of the bay listening to some seamen, I could picture the lonely cattle boats coming out of the north, stinking not of cattle, but of war, and bearing the scars of battle from out there beyond the rim. I could imagine how I, too, would have felt when none had news of the Randy. For somehow in everyone's mind, wrapped up with the disappearance of the luggers, was the mystery of the petrol and fuel dumps. Just how far north had Captain Fitzgerald planted those dumps? So far north that they weren't even in Australia?

Captain Fitz came and went, and came again to the lonely little port. And still there was no Randy. And he was inaccessible. No one could speak with him. He was immersed in papers, and the military police continually hovered about him.

Then a day came upon which a military personage arrived at the aerodrome, and invited Captain Fitz to accompany him somewhere into the blue sky, and there was consternation indeed in the town.

Captain Fitz had gone without farewell to anyone. His dinner was hot on the table at his bungalow, and his Chinese servant waited in vain for his master to come. The ink was undried on his pen, and he had not locked his cash-box. Captain Fitz had disappeared, like the luggers and the Randy, into the north.

Then the rumour came to the town. Captain Fitz had traded with the Japanese and had at last been arrested as a traitor. Would I have believed that rumour, I wonder? "Would I, if I had lived in Dampier and known the man and the ship as these people had known them, have lost faith as they lost faith? For lose faith they did.

After a little while the story got around that Captain Fitz had been sentenced to be shot, and that now all was over. They shrugged their shoulders when I asked them what they thought had happened to the Randy. I knew from the shamefaced laugh in their eyes that they had thought she was up there in the Banda Seas... with a yellow face at the helm. They had not cared, when they thought that, about the shooting of Captain Fitz. He had been cock of the walk too long, and now what was to become of the white inhabitants of Dampier marooned in a little northwest bay without fuel to give them means of departure? If Captain Fitz had sold the petrol to the Japanese, then good riddance to him!

They told me how time went on, and the news coming from Java and the islands to the north became more ominous. Soon there were only Timor and a string of islets between Australia and the oncoming yellow hordes. They, the people of Dampier, were bewildered. Where were the petrol and oil that meant power to the fighters lining the edges of the airfield? Where was the driving force for the transports? It was then that men really cursed the Randy and its captain. Shooting, they thought, had been too good for him.

And then came the wonderful morning.

When they came to this part of the story, the infectious laughter would well from their lips, and their eyes would shine. I, too, listening, felt the laughter rising in my heart for I knew what was coming. I knew, when they told me that dawn broke quietly with a whispered hush on that morning, and that the edge of the sea was pink and grey from the first touches of the sun rising across the red sand-hills in the east, I knew, before they said it, that when the light suffused the wide grey sea, there in the mists of the bay, would be the Randy.

And there too, they said, coming in on the tide, were all the luggers.

They told me how every man, woman and child came down to the edge of the bay and laughed and cried with delight, because they knew at once, that all those precious luggers carried oil, and not pearl shell. They knew, when they saw the Randy bristling with guns, that she had made that epic voyage through submarine-infested seas, under skies zooming with Japanese bombers, around the northwest hump of Australia to bring to Dampier the fuel it needed.

And all the while Captain Fitz was supposed to have been lying in a traitor's grave, he was, in reality, standing on the Randy's bridge shepherding the pearling fleet coming home with its cargo.

Yes, that was the best of all the things they told me in Dampier about the Randy and her skipper. How she and Captain Fitz must have shared their joke! They would have known full well what the townsfolk had been saying. They would guess that within an hour or two the same townsfolk would go about slapping one another on the shoulder and saying, "I told you so."

Ten days in all I had in Dampier. Ten wonderful, hot, sun-drenched days in the home of the Randy and her skipper. I felt closer than ever to the ship and my desire to find her burned almost like a fever.

"I don't know if this call has done you any good," said the mate. "It's made you feel the Randy's just around the corner. Well, she's no nearer to you, although you've been with people who have sailed in her. Maybe we'll pass her one night without ever knowing. While the war's on, you can't ask for news of her, and only luck would bring us into port together."

And the mate was sadly right. It was many a long day before I saw the Randy, but in all that long while, I never ceased to think and talk and dream about her.

CHAPTER IV

JOE

TIME had passed swiftly since the day Jeem died. First the weeks, then the months and after a while, a year or two slipped by, and the age of the atomic bomb had begun. The war was over, and I was nearly nineteen.

And yet war is not over so quickly as that. No one knows that better than the sailor. Maybe he no longer thinks of the danger of bombers and torpedoes, but there are always stray mines about. It may have seemed like peace in Australia, but we didn't see much of it whilst at sea. There was work to be done taking stores to the occupied islands in the Pacific, and there were a thousand and one islands in the seas between Darwin and Singapore where neither the Japanese nor the natives knew that war was at an end. Then, too, there was the seemingly endless business of cleaning up.

After a little while the ship I was with began the business of moving stuff from one-time war bases. It was thus I found myself again on the west coast of Australia.

I think this coast was destiny for me. The long

roll of the Indian Ocean and the voiceless reefs held the secret of a life that tantalised me with its lonely grandeur. I had known this coast all through my childhood, and now that I was growing to man's estate, I knew that whatever seas I sailed, to whatever strange lands I travelled, I would always be drawn again to the loneliness, the silence, the mystery of the seas that line the edge of the great continent.

And destiny brought our ship into the neighbourhood of Exmouth Gulf. Whilst the war was on, many of the islands between the gulf and the Abrolhos Archipelago were used as secret dumping grounds for submarine stores. We were engaged now in reloading much of this material and bringing it back to the coast of Australia.

We had come south past Dirk Hartog Island, and were heading towards Geraldton, when we were ordered to a small island well out from the straggling reef. There was no harbour, and the ship had to stand well to the west, and the working party went ashore in boats.

The first mystery to me was how a submarine could get inshore enough to use these stores, but once there ourselves, we discovered that this was no marine base. Through the centre of the island, and reaching from end to end, was a runway, and on the sheltered southern side were buoys. The island had been used for refuelling aircraft.

There was no one on the island now. It was as if ghosts had walked its scrub bypaths and left no sign of footprint or memory of human kind. The stores were there right enough, however, and there too, lay the long eerie windswept tarmac.

For two days we worked getting the material into dumps by the shore, and when most of it was ready to take aboard, the skipper, always a stickler for rules, ordered a watch party on shore for the night.

Volunteers were called for, and when I saw that the mate would take charge, I was quick to be amongst them. I had a longing to spend a night on the island, and I knew the mate would be the right company for me. We had to take water casks with us, and we weren't long in building a monster fire in the lee of the sandhills. The two men who accompanied us made a few caustic remarks about the skipper finding it necessary to set a watch, but the mate pointed with the stem of his pipe to the skyline.

"There are ships coming up," he said. "Two or three of them. They've been within wireless range for a day or two. They're American, and they'll be calling in round these parts themselves. A lot of that gear belongs to them." It was true that a great quantity of stuff was marked U.S.N., and we had had orders to leave it. The mate went on to enlighten us.

"The Americans are supposed to get their stuff at the same time as we get ours," he said. "Supposing they send a bunch of Chicago sailors ashore? What d'you think would happen to our stuff?"

"It would just about cut out evens if we landed a few Sydneysiders," said one of the men, Pederson he was called. The others laughed, while the mate took out his pipe and spat, and made no reply. I was huddling down by the fire and staring out into the blackness of the darkening sea. I knew that whatever the mate said about the Americans was only a cover-up. We neither of us could ever express what we felt about them since we'd been in Frisco.

After a little silence, he spoke again, but this time it was not of the Yanks, but of the Dutch.

"Somewhere down there among the islands in the south are six chests of silver," he said. "The Dutch left them there hundreds of years ago."

I heard the men stirring restlessly, and my own imagination flew into action at the very mention of the lost treasure. I knew the story of Pelsart's wrecking on the reefs and of how he had set out for Batavia in a pinnace in search of assistance. And of how, on returning, he found that the crew had mutinied and that there had been foul murder done, while the treasure of the wrecked ship had been mostly lost. I knew the story of how he had brought the remnants of the mutineers to trial there and then, and hanged in one batch all of them, except two, who had been marooned on one of the lesser islands. Listening while the mate retold the old story, I felt as if the ghosts of those two mutineers were stalking down the tarmac; as if I could hear their lone whispering in the whistling of the wind. What had become of them, I wondered. Had they ever found the mainland? Had they found human contact again... perhaps with the black people of Western Australia? What of Jeem, I wondered? Whence had he come? Could he have descended from those casta,ways? It was all fanciful thinking, I know, but somehow in keeping with the mood of the islands, with the shifting of the windswept sands beneath my hands, and with the strange night cry of a sea bird. "Those Luckless Abrolhos" Pelsart called the islands, and I knew that so long as the ghosts of the castaways talked in the wind, men would come here reluctantly, and would seldom stay.

My reverie was interrupted by the mate.

"Now, Ginge," he said. "It's just such a place as the Abrolhos that the Randy would find. And what a fine adventure it would be for her to take those six chests of silver out of the sea."

"They say that Pelsart's mutineers are still guarding the treasure," I said.

"Pooh," said the mate. "What are men dead three hundred years to a ship like the Randy?"

It was a nice thought, and even while the mate was talking, my mind was off on a possible adventure. What better than to fathom the secrets of the Abrolhos!

One of the men suddenly drew the mate's attention to some lights on the horizon. I, too, had just noticed them, and guessed them to be the ships that the mate had said were coming up. The lights appeared stationary now, and we guessed the ships were hove to.

"What d'you reckon they are?" asked Pederson.

The ship in the centre seemed larger; her line of lights was on a higher level than those of the two beside her.

"Maybe they're a couple of submarines," said the mate. "There's been a couple of American ones along the coast, calling in for a farewell or goodwill visit. There were a great many of them along this way after 1942. I guess the bigger ship is the one that is picking up the gear."

My thoughts went back to the sight of American and British submarines lying side by side in Fremantle, some battle scarred and some looking as if they would never see the deep sea again. And my thoughts went back with nostalgic longing to the day on the beach when two of us met the Americans, Joe, Sven and Ilka, and their story of the Randy. What, I had once asked the mate, had the Randy meant to Joe's imagination? Had he loved her, too, as he spun those thrilling yarns for two urchins on the shores of the Indian Ocean on a summer's day? But the mate had only shaken his head. He had not known Joe.

I felt him now poking me in the ribs, and I realised that he knew he had achieved his purpose when he bespoke the Randy for a treasure hunt in the Abrolhos. My heart was away with a lovely ship, and the mate was waiting for me to begin a yarn.

But strangely enough, the idea that I had in mind quite suddenly slipped away from me. My mind groped around for it. I thought of the ship, of Pelsart, of the Abrolhos, but it was as if there were some strange disturbance in my imagination, some force that would not let my thoughts group themselves together. Staring into the fire and sometimes looking away to the lights of the ships hove-to out of danger of the reefs, I tried vainly to build a story.

"What's the matter, Ginge?" asked the mate. "Randy let you down?"

"No," I said. "It just won't come."

As I spoke, I looked up and saw the lights of the smaller vessels wink and go out, leaving only one twinkling across the inky blackness of the sea.

"It's something to do with those subs," I said. "They've put a hoodoo on me tonight. I keep thinking about them."

"Well, never mind tonight, boy," said the mate. "We'll leave it for another time. It'll be better for keeping. Now you and Jeff can turn in. I'll call you for the late watch. And mind Pelsart's ghost don't go breathing down your ear funnels while you sleep."

I snuggled down in the sand, pulling my rug round me, and staring into the fire. Silence fell on the camp but for the occasional movement of the mate or Brown, who were on watch together.

Sometimes one or other got up and walked across the sandhills, or stood silhouetted against the moon, now rising out of the silvered sea.

It was near morning when the mate called me to take over, and I had to stamp the stiffness out of my legs by a smart run down to the sea's edge and back. The wind whipped my face, and I could tell by the strong smell of sea in it that weather was coming up out of the west. As the black of night paled to grey, I could see the deep banks of storm cloud on the western horizon, and I saw the black shapes of the American ships stealing round to the lee. In the half light of dawn they disappeared around the headland, and I was not then to see whether the mate's guess was right that there actually were two submarines with the ship.

Morning came, and it was cold. The wind was coming with a whip off the sea. There was nothing for it but to wake the mate and ask for instructions. The stores were exposed, and if the storm came down on them, there might be a lot to answer for. It took the four of us two hours' heavy going to get the stuff under some kind of cover, and we were barely in time. It seemed as if there was a body of black cloud to the nor' west billowing forth to meet a similar cloud mass from the sou' west, and it was inevitable that they would meet in a hurly burly overhead. We had only minutes to wait, before the wind came in like a raging tornado, whirling and tearing at the sea and land in a mad turmoil. It howled and whistled, and tore at the tufts of bush, stripping the scrub saplings of all but their thin spiry stems. It bashed at the sea and boiled it into a whirling cauldron. And then the rain came down as if the reservoirs of heaven had opened at that very spot.

It was over in half an hour, leaving a stripped and shivering island surrounded by grey angry seas.

"Cock-eyed Bob," said the mate. "First time I've been in one of them for years. Wonder how the ship took it?"

We were peering through the mists of rain for the sight of the ship, but she, like the Americans, had thought discretion the better part of valour, and had moved out to sea. The mate sent one of the men over the sandhills to see if he could sight any of the vessels, and we got to work to see how much damage had been done to the stores.

"Too many reefs round these parts," he said in excuse for having deprived us of the services of one man, even if only for a little while. "Cockeyed Bobs are not so good in reef seas."

We worked strenuously for a while, and presently the man came back to report that he could see four vessels wallowing unhappily in the distance. The Americans, he thought, were coming in closer to the island, and one of the submarines—they were subs after all—was leading the way.

There was too much to do to take a run round the headland or over the sandhills, and it was late afternoon before we got a boat from our own ship with instructions and some stores. We would have to stand watch again and when the seas had subsided in the morning, we could begin the business of loading the stuff on boats.

The mate still kept me hard at it, so that all that long, grey day, there was a ship lying off the island and I did not see her. I did not know that the lovely ship Dynar was at hand.

All that day I hauled at tarpaulins, heaved casks, stooped to wrenches, but all the time I knew there was something on the island like a spell. In the wind it was, and in the sighing and crying of the shattered grasses. And yet it was not a sadness.

The ghosts of Pelsart's mutineers, I thought. They cry, but not in terror. They have become part of the reeflands. They call in the winter wind, and on summer days, they grow quiet as the becalmed sea along the shore.

But it was not Pelsart's castaways that were disturbing the crying of the sea birds. It was the Dynar, and twelve hours more were to pass before I saw her.

Night came down on a calmer sea, but we built our camp well into the sand dunes, and I sat tired, but still restless within myself, watching the firelight flicker the shadows between the hillocks. Day had barely gone, and we had built our fire, and been sitting at it but a few minutes, when we heard a cry from the shore beyond the headland. It was resonant and deep, and we all knew at once that it was an American.

"I'm betting you," said the mate, "that some of the Yanks have landed."

"They don't have much space on those submarines," said Pederson. "They get shore-party leave wherever possible. I guess they've sent one or two ashore to try out the lie of the land, and to see just what the Britishers are up to."

Brown had given an answering shout, and gone over the sandhills to reach the beach. We could hear him now shouting a greeting to the Americans. Presently we heard the Americans talking with their sub through a megaphone.

And then there was the sound of men's boots thrashing in the undergrowth and of men's voices answering one another.

Then, high over the sand dune, came Brown, lurching a bit in the deep sand, and hitching his pants as was his habit. The moon came up over the quietening sea, edging the last of the cloud masses with silver.

The fire shot fiery tongues of light into the secret hollows between the dunes and over the hills came three figures. They stood there a minute, poised against the dark blue of the night sky, and then they came down through the wet sucking sand to the fire. They were speaking, but I could not hear them, for the hammering of my astonished heart. The mate was speaking too, but I could not hear him either. For over the hills had come Joe and Sven and Ilka!

CHAPTER V

THE RANDY

How brightly the flames of that camp fire licked into the sky that night!

Joe and Sven and Ilka stood beside it, their tapering forms in the blue of the American Navy silhouetted against the brilliance of the leaping light. I could hear them shouting names at one another, introducing themselves to the mate and Brown and Pederson, and our men laughing and talking back to them. And then they were all looking at me. It was as if the night beyond the fire circle was suddenly darker because of the silence.

"Wait a minute," said the mate. " Did you say *Joe* and *Sven* and *Ilka*?"

He looked at me, and I stood silent, and even my thoughts were incoherent. Here was the moment for which I'd waited years, and yet it found me unprepared.

"That's right, buddy." It was Joe's unmistakable voice.

"Say, Ginge, what's this?" said the mate starting forward. "Can these blokes be *your* Joe and Sven and Ilka?"

Before I could answer, Joe straightened himself up, and came round the fire and taking my shoulder in his great hand, spun me round so that the firelight shone on my face. He tilted my head forward with his other hand, and I knew he was looking at my hair.

"Ginge, by all that's holy," he said. He thrust out his jaw and brought his face close down to mine, at the same time tightening his grip on my shoulder, until it was all I could do to stop from crying out.

"You little red-headed rat," he said, and shook me. The anger in his voice shocked me back to reality. Whatever I had thought Joe would say to me when we met again, I had not dreamed it would be words of wrath. He turned to his companions. He seemed to have forgotten for a moment that there were others standing by.

"Just have a look-see at this. Look who's here," he said to Sven and Ilka, and he gave a strained kind of a laugh as if he were terribly angry.

"Say! Have I looked for that red-head or have I? The whole U.S. Navy is looking for him!"

He turned again to me. He was not such a tall man, but he was nearly a head taller than I. No one else but Joe could have called me a "redheaded rat" in spite of my few inches. I was nineteen now, and could pack a punch, but maybe Joe thought I was still that fifteen year old kid he had known at the bay. Maybe he went on thinking it, because I took what he was calling me. I took it because I knew there was something behind it, and I knew Joe.

"So the Randy's yours," he said, and there was contempt in his voice. "Yours to do what you like with—even to splash her name in two-inch letters across every newspaper in the country!"

"Take it easy," said the mate. "That happened two and a half years ago."

"What difference does that make?" asked Joe, "except that it's given me two and a half years to think about it. And to think what I'd say to him if I ever found him!" He swung round towards me again, and suddenly his hand shot out and seized my shoulder in a grip that hurt.

"I've been looking for you," he said slowly. "Looking everywhere. And I've had others looking too. Every time I heard that someone I knew was due to sail, I'd find him and say to him, 'Let me know if you come across a red-headed kid called Ginge who tells yarns about the Randy.' There are boys in boats going to Chile looking for you; they're looking for you on the London docks and up Shanghai way; they're looking in Sydney and Cape Town and Port Said. Wherever there are ships and harbours, wherever U.S. sailors go, they're looking for you. And why? you ask. So that I can deal with you!"

He stopped a minute and peered closely at me. It was as if he suddenly took stock of me and realised that I'd grown up.

"You're bigger," he said. "Perhaps they didn't find you because they were looking for a whippersnapper. And who'd have thought of finding you here, anyhow? Here, at the end of the world?"

Someone kicked the logs of the fire, and the flames leapt up anew. I could see the lights and shadows of Joe's face, and it didn't look any older to me.

"So you took the Randy," he went on, "and called it *your* Randy?" And though Joe was angry, deeply and terribly angry, I was only thinking of one thing. I was glad Joe felt that way about the Randy. I had never really known whether he loved her too. I was almost glad that he was mad at me.

From a long way away I summoned up my voice.

"I'm glad you feel that way, Joe," I said.

He shook me furiously for a moment, and then let me go.

"You're glad," he said. "Hear him! He's glad!" he

roared at Sven and Ilka. "Say, do you know I'm going to kill you? Kill you bit by bit, and throw you to the fishes? Do you know I've been looking for you two and a half years, and the whole U.S. Navy has been looking for you two and a half years for me to kill you?" He stopped short in front of me. "So what about that?"

"I'm glad you feel that way about the Randy, all the same," I said. "And I've been looking longer than two and a half years for you too, Joe. If I got over fond of the Randy you've got to remember that it was you who started it. You've got to remember that you once told the police back there in Perth that you had made up those yarns about the Randy, and I've been waiting much longer than two and a half years to ask you why."

Joe dropped to the ground. He sat hunching his head on his shoulders, and nobody said anything. Everybody just stood or sat and gazed at him and me, but nobody said a word.

Presently Joe's shoulders began to heave, and after a minute, I knew he was laughing. Huge gusts of laughter shook him, and I knew that his rage was gone. As suddenly as he dropped to the ground, he stood up and faced Sven and Ilka.

"I ask you," he said. "What do you think of him?"

Sven shifted the gum in his mouth, and kicked a

log into the fire. Ilka took his gum out and rolled it into a neat little ball between his thumb and forefinger.

"I kind of like him," he said.

"Me too," said Sven.

I had a feeling all along that they weren't against me, but Joe was different. I suppose the Randy was his ship in the sense that he was the first to tell stories about her; and I had got it streamed in headlines across the American papers. He was entitled to feel as he did, and I told him so. And then he began to laugh again in a quiet, considering way.

"It wasn't only that, buddy," he said. "It was the way you nearly mucked things up after that pal of yours went west up there at the bay."

There was a momentary silence, and for the first time, I wondered what Brown and Pederson were thinking. They knew I had something of a reputation for spinning yarns, and they knew that most of my yarns centred around the Randy, but they knew nothing of my early history, nor of the bay, nor of Jeem. It was the mate who broke the silence.

"Well, seeing that there's going to be no killing after all, and no feeding to the fishes, let's settle down and brew a billy of tea." There was a sudden relaxation of the tension, and everyone began to busy himself doing something around the fire. Pederson produced the billy, and out of the Americans' pockets came some tinned corn. Brown began to mix a damper, and within a few minutes, he was turning it in the coals. I still said nothing because I couldn't get over the feeling of anticipation that now, at long last, I was to know why Joe had denied his friendship with me on that day nearly four years ago when we had been in the Police Commissioner's office.

After we had eaten some damper and corn, and were sipping the boiling tea, the mate filled his pipe, while the Americans shook cigarettes from their packets.

"You know, Joe," said the mate. "Ginge and I have been together ever since he came to sea. He's told me about the bay, and I too, would like to know what was behind that denial of yours. Is there any reason why the story should not be told now?"

"No," said Joe. "The war's over and done with. And it's a war story." I could hear everyone settling down in the sand, but I felt myself leaning forward. Every nerve in my body was taut.

"I suppose he's told you what the Randy was doing along this coast in those days. She'd take out a big supply of fuel, and we—that is, the subs—would go straight up Singapore way. Our fuel would carry us out, but we would have to have a rendezvous with the Randy to get enough stuff to get back. Sometimes the Randy would sneak through without any trouble. The skipper knew her every mood, and what's more, he knew every islet and lagoon from the Timer Sea to Tokio. When she was empty, back she'd come to Fremantle for supplies, sometimes with us in tow, and sometimes on her own. Well, there was a blackout along the west coast in those days, but the lookout reckoned a couple of times that there was a pinpoint of light ashore about fifteen or twenty miles north of the port. It was reported, and some kind of a patrol went up there, but there was nothing sighted. What's more, we three were the only others who could see that light. Maybe me and Sven and Ilka and the lookout on the Randy had been fed on carrots when we were kids, and we could see more than most people at night. It got to be quite an argumentative point, that light. On shore they reckoned there was no such thing, and nearly all our guys agreed with them.

But it began to get us down. We hadn't been such buddies before, but as each of us was certain he could see a light, we sort of got together on the point.

"One time when we were in Fremantle, we had shore leave, and we went up that way to have a look-see for ourselves. That's when we saw the surfing carnival at a place called Benson Beach. That's when we first met Ginge. I told him about the Randy. That was my first big mistake." Joe paused for a while, and again I could hear the others stirring as they altered their positions in the sand.

"He was dead serious, that kid. I should have known I was playing with dynamite when I wound him up about the Randy. But I like a good yarn myself, and I had a kind of fellow-feeling for him. You should have seen his eyes popping." The mate gave a chuckle and threw a small handful of sand at me. After that I relaxed a bit, and found myself crouching down in the cold sand, and gazing not at Joe, but into the coals of the friendly fire.

"Well," Joe went on. "The Randy went out that day, and we'd arranged with the lookout that if he saw the light, he was to give us the tiniest flicker. If he didn't see anything, they'd go out all black. Well, we stayed that night on Benson Beach, and sure enough, we caught the tiniest flicker when the Randy must have been about seven miles further north than we were. About two miles north of us was another holiday resort called Blackman's Bay, and after that, there was nothing but endless beach for hundreds of miles. We snooped around Blackman's Bay, and found that the reason why there was no one further north was because there was sup-posed to be no water there. After a while, we got it out of someone that there was a legend that there had been a half-blooded tribe up that way, and that they must have had a secret water hole... but it seemed as if it was only legend.

"Well, me and the boys went back to the sub, and we put it to the C.O. that we were certain sure there was someone up that way. It was no good making complaints to the authorities, so the skipper gave us leave to have a look around unofficially. That day the sub went out of Fremantle without Sven and Ilka and me. We went straight up to Blackman's Bay. The first day we set out on our errand, we saw where someone—maybe only a kid—had gone alone up that beach. We followed where he left footprints along the hardened edge just out of reach of the surf line. Those footprints belonged to Ginge. When we got to the Bay we found him and his little half-caste pal. A boy named Jeem."

Joe's voice died away for a minute. I felt a lump in my throat, for as he talked, I lived again that long walk from my father's cottage to the bay. I saw again, through Joe's eyes, the picture of me and Jeem lying on the sand the day that Joe and Sven and Ilka had rounded that southern promontory and come towards us.

"As soon as we knew about Jeem," said Joe, "we knew about the light. The light we used to see at sea was Jeem's light. Poor little chap... he didn't even understand that there was a war on, or what it was about. He'd never mixed with the whites, though his people must have done so once, for he spoke English. And he couldn't understand why he couldn't have a light. After Ginge used to go home at sundown, we'd set to work to track Jeem to his bumpy hut, but he was as shrewd as any blackfellow. He knew when he was being tracked, and he'd give us the slip. What we couldn't understand was why he never admitted in the morning that he knew we'd been after him. And he never told Ginge here. We never told him either, because he returned each night to the town, and we couldn't afford to run the risk of his giving the show away. You see, this game of hide and seek we were having with Jeem, made us pretty suspicious that there was something more to it than just a camp fire at night, and Jeem played dumb by day just the same as we did."

Joe stopped here. I felt that what he had to say next, was going to be painful listening, and that he was gaining time by the excuse of shaking himself out another cigarette and lighting it with more than necessary formality.

"And there *was* something more to it. We weren't the only ones who'd seen Jeem's light. The Japs had. That was why Jeem was evading us. He had to light his camp fire, and he had to do it in a different place every night. But we caught up with him in the end. That goes without saying. It wasn't till we caught him that we were able to get the story out of him. I suppose it would be hard for you fellows to realize that a young'un could live alone on that beach, and not know what he was doing when he contacted the Japs. And yet that's precisely what happened. When we got Jeem's story out of him, it was this. Blackout or no blackout, he lit his fire as usual. One morning at dawn he was awakened by the sound of someone coming stealthily towards his humpy. When he sat up, there was a small brown man standing over him. It was a Jap, as we knew when Jeem described him. The Jap soon satisfied himself that Jeem lived there alone, that he was part-native, and that he knew little or nothing of the war except that many, many ships now sailed up and down the Roads. Jeem said that there were two Japs, and that after they had spoken with him, and got water from his waterhole, they got into a little boat... only just big enough for the two of them. And that they closed the roof of the little boat over their heads, and that it then went under the water. If you remember that all this was before we knew anything of the midget submarines, you can guess why we didn't quite believe Jeem. If we had only done so, we might have saved him from death.

"The Japs made an appointment with Jeem to come again, and he was to keep a count of the ships that went out of the harbour, and to keep them classified into sizes. But above all, he was to watch for the Randy. They drew a picture of her for Jeem, and he recognised it, for he had already known the Randy, and had watched for her often. The Japs wanted a tally on her because they knew she was the ship supplying the fuel to the submarines that went far afield. They wanted those two subs particularly, and they wanted the Randy particularly. Her skipper knew more about the archipelagoes in the north than any other man on the seven seas. His knowledge and the daring of the subs, were doing more damage than any other combination of allied ships.

"And Jeem was faithfully keeping this tally. He just didn't know what he was doing. Even after we explained, he tried to persuade us that he had made these Japs a promise, and that he had to keep it. It wasn't until we made him believe that the Randy itself would be in danger that we won him over to our side. What we should have done was to persuade him to come south with us and tell his story to the military headquarters. What made us decide against that, was the fact that the Japs were due back, and we were afraid of losing them. Also, we were a bit doubtful about Jeem's story of the two-man submarine, and we wanted to test it out. We finally hit upon the plan of the three of us hiding out at the reef and letting Jeem keep his appointment with the Japs. The idea was that if there were only two of them we could pot them off from ambush with the pistol and Sven's knife.

"What we didn't bargain for, was that Jeem would tell them that he couldn't keep his promise, because he had three friends staying on the beach with him who had made him promise otherwise. At least that is what he must have told them. Sven and Ilka were hiding nearest among the jags of reef and saw the little sub emerge from the water. It was a midget all right. Jeem spoke to the man who came out of it and turned and pointed towards the beach. Before anything else could happen, the man had lifted his pistol and shot Jeem in the back of the head. In a second he was back in the sub, and as it was obvious that we could do nothing with the knife and pistol, we had to lie there helpless and watch it submerge."

I found my voice at last.

"So it wasn't a rock that made that hole in the back of his head?"

"No," said Joe. "The Jap got him."

There was a long silence.

"We just couldn't tell you, Ginge. There was something of the hero-worshipper about you. We couldn't tell you what Jeem had done—even though we knew he didn't realise what he was doing."

The mate cleared his throat.

"I suppose the midget submarine was a military secret, and that is why there was all that secrecy in the Commissioner's office."

"That's it," said Joe. "Intelligence closed down on it like a trap. We couldn't break the news to any living soul... not even to the Police Commissioner. As far as Ginge was concerned, he got a rough deal. The doctor had got his case all tied up in a bag anyway, and his father fell for a likely tale." He paused again, and then turned to me. "You know, Ginge, I was downright sorry for you until I saw you'd been at it telling yarns about the Randy all over the world and getting your picture in the papers in the U.S. Then I was just raving mad. Heck! I'm going to start and get mad all over again."

"Joe," I said. "Didn't *you* make up yarns about the

Randy? Not all the things you told us there at the bay were true, were they?"

"Yes," he said. "I made up a few yarns about her. But I always called her the Randy... it didn't matter much when no one really knew her real name."

"Her real name?"

"Yes," he said. "The Dynar. Out there..." he turned and pointed across the headland.

"The Dynar... out there?" I almost started up. Could it be? Could it be that the Randy was lying out there?

"Sure," said Joe, with an expression of surprise in his voice. "Didn't you know? Heck, she's been there since yesterday."

How could he know that I had not once seen the vessels lying off the island—that I didn't know that the Dynar was the Randy.

"Dynar!" said the mate thoughtfully.

"Yep, Dynar," said Joe. "She's the Randy. Transpose the first two letters, and then spell it out from the end. Y . . D . . N . . A . . R. It's R . . A . . N . . D . . Y back to front."

I said nothing. I don't think I even moved. Beyond the fire circle the night was black with a silver arch where the moon slid its pale way between the cloud banks. The mate came round the fire, and I felt his arm rub, as if by accident, against mine. His voice broke the spell with its matter of factness.

"Well, Ginge," he said. "We've just about had a day of it. What with the cock-eyed Bob, the stores, and now Joe with the Randy, we've had enough." He stretched his arms and yawned loudly. But Joe was embarked on one of his talking moods, and no hints from the mate would stop him. The night was still young after all. Gradually Joe's words began to take form, and sense, and I found myself listening again. Everyone was sitting or lounging round the fire. Even the mate gave up, and sat down beside me. Joe's voice went on and on.

"She knows every islet and broken reef from Timor to Tokio," he was saying. "Remember, Sven, the time we'd finished an assignment up in the north Pacific and were crawling down between the islands. We were empty. We hadn't enough oil to take us anywhere we knew. We couldn't have submerged if we'd wanted to. Then, in and out between the atolls came the Randy. Boy, did we cheer! She was always there... right at the crucial moment. And sometimes she'd turn up with all her guns smoking, and part of her upper works still smouldering. Maybe she'd shot her way through, or maybe she'd gone after some prey of her own. After a while we got to know she'd always turn up. We reckoned she knew the north. She didn't have to have any skipper or crew. She'd find her way."

"Got a nose of her own, eh?" asked Pederson.

"She's got everything," said Joe. "What a ship! She's officially listed as the Dynar, but Randy suits her best."

After a little while the talk grew desultory as the warmth of the fire and food and tea coursed through our veins, and one by one the men sank back on the sand, and began to fall asleep.

The mate rose and stretched himself again.

"Care for a stroll before we turn in?" he asked Joe. There was something in his voice that puzzled me, and it seemed to puzzle Joe too, because he looked quietly back at him for a moment, and then stood up without speaking, and walked with him into the darkness.

They were away quite a while, and the others were all asleep before I heard them coming back. They weren't talking much, but their voices sounded as if they liked each other, and when I saw their faces by the glow of the firelight, they were both smiling.

"Well, Ginge, what about it?" said the mate to me. "I've got a hunch you won't be sleeping tonight. Maybe you'd like to take the watch sitting up on that sandhill where you can see a certain ship as soon as dawn comes."

"Yes," I answered. The mate was always right. What made him so understanding about what was in a fellow's mind?

"Well, just to show there's no ill feeling, I'll go up with you," said Joe, and he jumped up and, coming round the fire, cuffed my head in a friendly way. I remembered how he used to do that at the bay, and when he said, "Up to the hill! Atta boy!" his voice sounded the same, too.

Up there on the ridge of the sand dune, we talked, and sometimes dozed, the night through. Now that the others weren't there, I could talk of the Randy to Joe. I told him how I had dreamed of only one thing, and that was of finding the ship again, and perhaps of one day joining her crew.

"She's U.S. Navy," said Joe. "It mightn't be so easy."

In the last four years all my wishful thinking had been so directed towards finding the Randy, that I had not given heed to the fact that as a naval ship, an ordinary seaman would not be able to join her. Now my joy in the anticipation of seeing the Randy again was a little spoiled by the fear that I might be only seeing her for a few hours, and that then she would sail away again without me.

We were silent for a long while. Sometimes I thought

I could see her shadow in the waters between silver troughs of sea as the moon cleared her way from behind the cloud banks and shone clear and silver over the surging ocean.

It was Joe who broke the silence.

"Does it mean so much to you, boy?" he asked. I nodded.

Words didn't come easily to me just then. But Joe seemed to understand.

"The mate talked to me a lot just now," he said. "He told me how you wanted to fight that reporter. I'd like to have a go at him myself. It was his paper I minded; the others didn't matter. I'm sorry, Ginge... I guess I didn't understand that you could feel that way about the Randy, too."

I nodded, and Joe lit a cigarette. For a long time we sat there without talking, but it was a good silence, and I knew that Joe and I were friends from now on, even if the Randy sailed away forever tomorrow... But I couldn't help wishing desperately that I could sail with her too.

When Joe did speak, it was about something else altogether.

"What do you do on that old tub of yours when there's someone ill, or badly hurt?" he asked. "Have you got a doctor on board?"

"No, we haven't," I said. "They either get better, or we put them off at the nearest port."

"What about a pharmacist's assistant?" asked Joe.

I shook my head.

"That's a member of the crew that U.S. ships carry," I said, "but there's no one like that on a tramp. Men have just got to take a chance when they ship on our type of tub. Once we had to stop in mid ocean and put a man off who'd broken his back. A British destroyer took him aboard. I don't know what happened to him."

Joe went on talking about other things for a while, and it was after that that we began to doze.

Just before dawn, Joe stirred sleepily.

"Hey, Ginge! You awake?"

"Yes," I said. "I've been awake some time now. I want to watch the light coming over the ocean, and see if the Randy is the way I pictured her." I also felt indescribably sad, for to see her now would be like looking upon forbidden fruit. What good was it to me to find the Randy, if I could not board her.

"She won't let you down," said Joe.

We stood up and stretched our legs. We stamped the cold out of them and beat ourselves with our hands to get the circulation going.

A grey line of light showed on the eastern sky, and

the blackness of the heavens lightened. The stars grew dim, and faded one by one. The wind off the sea curled round our ankles, and the grasses sighed. The four vessels hove-to off the island gradually took shape. I did not look at our own ugly ship. I did not look at the submarines. I looked at the Dynar, which was the Randy, and the dawn broke with a sigh, and out of the dark shadows, she rode like a ship in a dream.

She was as I had always known her in my fantasy. A long ship... keen and sharp, yet with an indolent air. She rode the grey waters like a seabird, gleaming, with the pearl mists of morning fading back from her. She was lovely as the morning itself.

I felt a lump in my throat. At long last, I thought, this is the Randy. My Randy.

I heard Joe stoop behind me, and even in my rapt dream, some instinctive premonition warned me. I half turned, and caught one second's glance from Joe's face. His lips were drawn back, and there was a peculiar light in his eyes. His face was grim. He wasn't looking at the Randy. He was looking at me.

I saw all that in a split second; then his hand with something in it came up in a swift upward jerk behind me.

For one instant I felt as if the back of my head

had been stove in, and then there was blackness and nothingness.

When I awoke, I was first aware of the creak of ship's timbers beneath me, and of the soughing of water past the gunwales. The back of my head ached intolerably.

Then I remembered that Joe had struck me. Joe, I thought. Joe! I must have said his name out aloud, for someone leaned over me.

"Joe's just gone on deck," he said.

"On deck?"

"Yes. You've had a crack on the head. Joe said there was no M.O. on your ship, so he brought you here. You're on the Dynar."

"The Dynar?" I said. "You mean the Randy?"

"Okay, if it suits you that way," he laughed. "Here comes the doctor now. Just hold steady."

As the doctor stooped over me, I was more conscious of the deck beneath me than of the man above me. My hand was sliding over the boards, and I was thinking. "This is the Randy. I'm on board the Randy."

"How'd that happen?" asked the doctor, feeling with light fingers around the back of my head.

"Just an accident," I mumbled.

"Joe and his two buddies brought him on board,"

said the first man who had spoken to me. "Said the kid has fainting spells, and needs a bit of attention. The skipper on his own ship is quite anxious for us to take him along. That's if you think it necessary, doc."

The doctor hummed and hawed for a while, and then looked closely at me, and if ever anyone prayed hard, I prayed then.

"All right," he said. "We'll take him along."

When the doctor had gone, I sat up and held my poor head in my hands. Then I looked up towards the bridge.

"Is Captain Fitz up there?" I asked.

"He sure is, kid," said the sailor. "You couldn't part him from the Randy!"

So I had found the dream at last, and the dream was good. "Will you give Joe a message from me?" I asked at length.

"I sure will, kid. Anything you say!"

"Just tell him that everything's all right," I said slowly... "That's all there is to say!... Everything's *all right*!"